JINETERA

Story of a Cuban prostitute

YOUSI MAZPULE

JINETERA

Story of a Cuban prostitute

Published by Eriginal Books LLC
Miami, Florida
www.eriginalbooks.com
eriginalbooks@gmail.com

First: Edition March 2012

ISBN-13: 978-1-61370-984-9
Library of Congress Control Number: 2012935523

CHAPTER ONE

Before my mother tried crossing the Florida Straits on a raft made out of inner tubes, she and I slept on the twenty-year-old velvet mustard couch that was the only piece of furniture left in the house. The air from the two fans, the only electrical appliances left, was thick and humid. I could barely breathe and tossed and turned until dawn, when I finally fell into a light sleep for about an hour before waking up to the smell of warm milk and coffee that my mother always circled near my nose.

"Milena here's your café con leche, mi hija," she whispered.

I, not wanting to wake up to the last day I'd spend with my mother, feigned sleep.

"I know we won't see each other for a while," she started after a deep breath, "but we'll be together in a big house in Miami sooner than you think." The sun was just beginning to show its face on the new day.

"I'm almost seventeen, mami, why can't I just come with you?" I said getting up to take my café con leche.

"I'm not going to put my only daughter in danger, I've told you that. You have to stay, finish your school, and in less than six months you'll be in Miami with me."

"I don't want to stay in Cuba by myself."

"You won't be by yourself. You have your tia, your cousins..."

"She doesn't even like me," I said, and took a long sip.

"She loves you, she's just not good at showing her feelings..." she said getting up. As she sieved the coffee grounds through the men's sock that was our coffeemaker, I thought about the last two years; how she had tried to leave the country by different venues. None worked. Because she was a professional dancer, she could take a plane to any Latin American country with the dance company, but the government wouldn't let her take me.

"I don't want to live with Tia Susi, mami; I want to be with you."

"I know, mi amor, but I'll send her dollars from the U.S. so she could take care of you. And things will be easier here with dollars."

She reassured me things would be fine in less than six months, and that that was all the time she needed to reunite me with her. Three months before, during an extensive investigation in Costa Rica on what she was doing at the American embassy when she was supposed to have met Cuban officials at Juan Santamaria Airport and taken a plane back to Cuba shortly after, I had stayed with my aunt Susi.

"Tia Susi thinks I steal her food. She's paranoid."

"Milena everybody lives like that on this island!"

"I want to go with you. Please take me with you," I

said crying and running to hug her backside. She let go of the coffee in the sink, turned and hugged me tight. We both tried to hold back the tears the entire morning.

But at noon, when it was time for her to get on the bus that would take her to the bay where she would wait until the sun went down to get on the raft, she got on her knees in front of the door, crossed herself crying, and said a quick prayer. She signaled for me to do the same. Besides the Holy Father, which was the only prayer we knew, I didn't know how else to ask for my mother not to leave. So I didn't; I stood there, looking at her on her knees, hair pulled back into her traditional ballerina bun, her spine straight like the palm trees that populated the city. I cried in silence knowing that if I let go of the composure she had begged me to keep three nights before when I had thrown myself on the floor bawling like a five year old in a fit of rage, she wouldn't go anywhere. I knew she needed to go.

The early nineties were deemed a "special period" by the regime and life had become twice as difficult for us since my mother's attempt to defect in San Jose. Food was difficult to get without dollars, and because she was now on the list of anti-revolutionaries, she had been dismissed from her job. The bodeguero assigned to the distributing center we got our meager portions from had usually been willing to give her a few dollars for any jewelry or double the amount of chavitos--the new currency the government had invented--she gave him. But he told her he was a member of the committee for the defense of the Revolution, and could no longer risk his position to help her. And our neighbors had been kind to us until a month ago when a sign was posted on our door that announced we had been re-assigned to another section of town; a section my mother said she'd rather die than live in.

The raft never made it. They found pieces of it in Palm Beach. There had been six people on that raft. No bodies were found. Two months before I turned seventeen, I went from the town of Regla to a tenement in La Habana Vieja to live with my mother's half-sister. Tia Susi made it clear from the beginning that I had to somehow earn my keep. Times were hard and she couldn't provide for me and her two small children.

"I can offer you a roof to sleep under," she said when I arrived at her house. "But when the meat and milk comes once a month, I have to give that to my kids. You need to find a way to make dollars to help me out with the household expenses."

The distribution of food corresponding to each month was twenty ounces of red or black beans, half a liter of oil, one pound of a meat/soy mixture, one pound of texturized ground meat, two pounds of rice, one liter of milk per child under the age of seven, and occasionally one full chicken was given to the most revolutionary family on the block. The rest had to be bought in what according to the government, was a non-existent black market.

Tia Susi was an unhappy woman in her mid-forties who had had kids late in life. She was the product of my maternal grandfather's first wife and had not been close to my mother at all until their father had died two years ago. My mother had tried to foster a relationship with her big sister, but it was strained, and one sided. My tia had not been too enthused about having to share the scarce personal belongings her father had left her with a half-sister her mother had taught her to hate.

The solar she lived in was in the corner of Montes and Cienfuegos avenues, an area known for drugs and street prostitutes that were not just for tourists as in other parts of La Habana. The apartments, most of them originally of two and three bedrooms with living and dining room areas, had been reduced to just one or two rooms that became the bedrooms at night and the living spaces during the day.

Two families of four could live in one of the apartments all sharing the bathroom and the kitchen. Luckily, Tia Susi had two rooms just for her and the kids, and while we still had to share the bathroom with other families, the sleeping arrangements were not so bad considering what the other families had.

I slept in a cot in one of the rooms with the kids while my aunt slept in the other room with whoever the boyfriend was for the night. Through the windows, I could hear people outside smoking, drinking, arguing.

The kids would wake up, look out from under the sheet that covered the window, and stare for hours at the goings-on outside.

"Niños, let's go to sleep," I'd say to them. "You two shouldn't be looking at all that." But they'd say, "Our mother lets us, so who are you to tell us not to." I'd just cover my head with the thin sheet and try to sleep.

The solares were the ghettos of La Habana. Beautiful apartment buildings in Batista's time, now all that was left were trash covered courtyards with doors to the apartments that had no handles, no locks, no paint on them. The windows were covered with aluminum foil or sheets, curtains or shades were a luxury few could afford. The smells of the solares were a mixture of years of water damage that had seeped into the walls mixed with overused frying oils, human waste and sweat. And because they were severely overcrowded, there was no telling from which unit the smells came; it was the overall smell of La Habana condensed within a few decaying walls.

By the time rations came, I had not eaten a piece of meat in over a month. The two pounds of meat per family were supposed to be delivered to the bodegas on a monthly basis. Sometimes meat didn't come for two or three months, and when it did, only families with children could claim the rations first. I had no nucleus, meaning parent and offspring, to claim as a family anymore. And my libreta-the ration booklet that needed to be stamped in order to receive the goods-had disappeared with the rest of my mother's valuable things.

My mother left me her two gold rings and a pair of pearl earrings, $400 dollars she had saved, and the libreta. But I was a minor, and only an adult could claim the food rations. The jewelry and the money, no one had seen since the day after she left when the Defense Committee of the Revolution came into our tiny apartment and asked me to collect my things, the state was claiming all of my mother's property. Tia Susi said all of my mother's things were probably at the bottom of the ocean along with her bones.

My cousins were five and seven, the boy and the girl respectively, and the two gallons of milk that was distributed went in less than two weeks. One of the many chores I had to do to "earn my keep" was to make their café con leche in the mornings and take them to school while my tia slept. One morning, the boy cried for more leche with his café. I told him there was none and he ran to his mother to complain.

"Did you drink the milk?" My aunt asked accusingly, though barely awake.

"No, I don't really like milk."

"But you like café con leche."

"Yes, but I have it with evaporated milk. I would never drink their milk."

"Umph," she scoffed. "If I find that you drank the milk, you're gonna be out of here before you can even say your full name."

I was already getting used to her accusing me of anything that went wrong in the house. The rice and malanga she bought with dollars was also gone by the end of the week. I ate old stale bread and drank faucet water for days.

On a warm early August evening, my aunt's friend came over with rabo, oxtail cooked in tomato sauce. Tia Susi felt sorry for me and gave me some of the leftover sauce to scrape with some bread. There was a piece of fried steak in the fridge she had been saving for the kids, and she threw it in the saucer with the tomato sauce. I cleaned the bottom of the pan with some more bread. It had been nearly a week since I had had a decent bite to eat.

The steak had sat in the fridge for too long, and given the daily scheduled power outages that lasted no less than two hours, had begun to rot. I spent the entire night throwing up and running to the toilet with diarrhea. In the morning, I was dehydrated and couldn't get up from bed. My aunt's friend took me to the hospital where I sat in a dilapidated room with three other women--one of them in labor--for four hours before anyone called my name.

After some blood work, it was determined I had bacterial poisoning from the steak. I spent the night in the hospital. The woman who had been in labor shared the room with me. I watched her watch her baby's peaceful sleep the entire night.

I could not fall asleep. My stomach turned into painful knots. I got up at least five times to run to the toilet. The nurse had left a bucket at my bedside and instructed me to ring the bell behind me if I needed her. I rang and rang. She never came. When the doctor came into the room at almost noon the next day, he checked the new mom first. She had low blood sugar and blood pressure, and had to stay at least one more day. I was still somewhat dehydrated, although my strength was coming back slowly. The doctor, who had a balding head and thick spectacles, asked me if I felt strong enough to go home.

"Is anyone here to pick me up?" I asked.

"No," the nurse answered.

I didn't have any money for a taxi, and the idea of catching a bus stuffed with sweaty people didn't seem appealing at the moment.

"I really don't feel strong enough to leave."

"I'll come back tomorrow to see how you're doing," the doctor said, signaling for the nurse to change my IV.

When she was done, I looked over at the girl with the new baby. I said hello and told her my name. She said hers was Kassandra.

"With a K," she said. "My mother thought that was how the Russians spelled it."

"Is it?"

"I don't know. If that was how the Yankis spelled it, then it would matter," she answered.

We spent hours talking about the labor and the horrible conditions of the hospital, among other things. Kassandra was a pretty and naturally red-headed girl of about twenty who was obsessed with anything from the United States. La Yuma, los Yankis or el norte was all she talked about, and how she wanted her daughter to grow up in Miami, not in La Habana.

"In la Yuma, she can study something, she can be somebody, she can have whatever she wants. I want her to have a better life than mine."

Then she started to cry. I mustered up all the energy I had to drag myself with the IV to her side of the room to sit on the edge of the bed. She hugged me while she cried for a good ten minutes. I just patted her back and assured her things would be fine for her and the baby.

"Things will never be fine here." She wiped her face with her hospital gown. "If I don't leave this country, things will never be good for my daughter."

"My mother used to say that all the time," I said.

I told her how my mother always said she would do anything for me to grow up in la Yuma. She was one of the best dancers in the world-renowned cabaret Tropicana. She had been to Mexico, Costa Rica, Panama, but always with the dance company. She was terrified when two Cuban officials came to her hotel room in Panama City to inform her that she would never see me again if she even thought about defecting. From Miami, it was easier to legally claim me or come back for me; she could hire someone who owned a boat, or a small plane, and once our feet touched ground in the US, there was be nothing the Cuban government could do.

After a long pause, Kassandra said, "I'm a jinetera. That's why I tell you that if I don't get her out of here, she'll turn out just like me."

"You're a prostitute for the tourists?"

"Yes," she said looking into my eyes. Unashamed.

"I can't raise her here." Again a piercing look from her green eyes. Now ashamed.

"That doesn't necessarily have to be the case," I said. "She can grow up to be anything she wants anywhere in the world."

"Under Castro? How old are you again?"

"Almost seventeen."

"Most girls I know your age are already doing what I do for a living."

"How long have you been a jinetera?"

"Since I was twelve, maybe thirteen, can't remember. My mother was a fletera; her clients weren't tourists but the sailors on cargo ships from all over the world. Her mother was a fletera as well. I come from a long line of whores, you know," she said with a smirk. "If I stay here, she'll be on the streets by eleven."

We both looked over at the rotting wooden bassinet. Kassandra's face, although breathtakingly beautiful, was missing the freshness of youth, the irreproachability of twenty. She cried every time she looked at her daughter.

"Why don't you just stop doing it?"

"I don't know how to do anything else. And you can't just stop."

"Why not?"

"Because...well...I've never..." she took a deep breath. "I've thought a lot about not doing it anymore, but I can't just make that decision on my own."

"What about your family? They can help you."

"I don't have a family. I have a chulo and he would

never let me quit."

The word chulo meant something cute, like a little boy with a cute outfit was chulo to me. But on the street, a chulo was a man who ran a group of jineteras, a pimp who provided the girls with protection in exchange for half their wages.

"He takes half your money?"

"Sometimes he takes it all if he needs it for a business deal. When he feels generous he only takes half."

"That doesn't seem fair. You're the one doing all the work."

"That's just how it is. His father was my mom's pimp, and I don't know any further back, but from what he tells me, his family has been in this business for some time."

"Sounds like a wonderful guy." I said.

"He's not that bad but..."

I waited for her to finish the sentence. She didn't. The nurse came in to check on us. We hadn't realized the sun was coming up and Kassandra soon fell into a light sleep. The baby slept without making a sound. I tried to but it wasn't until hours later that I actually fell asleep.

The baby's wailing woke me from the deepest sleep I had had in months. For a few seconds I was disoriented and didn't know where I was. I could recall a faint dream of being on a boat with my mother. But as I looked around the decaying walls, the old hospital equipment, and at Kassandra struggling with the baby in her arms, reality set in. The windows, covered by obsolete curtains from the sixties that were not very good at keeping the sun out, had steel bars running on the outside, like a photo I had seen of a mental institution in an American movie.

"She's so hungry but she won't take my breast," Kassandra said.

"Call the nurse."

"I did. Five times already!"

I took a deep breath in order to gather strength to pull myself up. I pressed my nurse button continuously for a good minute or so.

"What's going on here? You two are going nuts with those buttons," the nurse yelled charging in a few minutes later.

"The baby won't stop crying," I told her.

"That's what babies do, my dear. And premature babies cry even more."

"Premature?" I looked at Kassandra. "I didn't know she was premature."

"Only a few weeks," she said, looking down at her baby.

"A few weeks too many. She should've stayed in her mom's belly for at least another six weeks," the nurse continued as she took the baby from Kassandra's arms. "So expect her to be a troublesome baby."

"If she's premature, shouldn't she be in an incubator?" I asked. I had read this information in one of the magazines my mother had brought me from Mexico.

"We only have four of them in the hospital, and there were three other premature births with a lot more risk."

"What about the fourth? Can't she be put in there?" I said.

"It was occupied until this morning. But now I'm going to feed her, and put her in until the doctor comes later on."

Kassandra kissed her baby's forehead before the nurse took her. "My baby has been alive for over twelve hours, and is only now they are going to give her some medical attention. And you think she'll get a fair shot at life here? She's already starting on the wrong foot."

"She looks very strong. There's nothing you can do about her wanting to come earlier than planned." I said, trying to sound reassuring while knowing nothing about babies.

"My boyfriend slapped me and I fell, and when I hit my stomach on the floor, I went into labor."

"The baby's father slapped you?"

Kassandra looked away. "I'm not sure he's the father. I told him I had been with a Yuma without using a condom and that I wasn't sure this was his baby."

"He knows what you do?"

"He's my chulo."

"Why would you have this baby if you didn't know whose it was?"

"I used to think he loved me and that this would change him."

"If he really loved you, he wouldn't have slapped you," I said.

"You ever been in love?"

"No," I said, hearing my mother's voice saying that if a man really loves you, he would never use his hands to hurt you. I told Kassandra the story my mom had told me of how my own father had doubted I was his, and offered to pay for the abortion when she told him she was pregnant. My mother said no and threatened to go to the authorities if he didn't accept responsibility for his actions. He was a high ranking general of the Revolution, married with two older kids. If word got out that he had been with one of the young mulata dancers from Tropicana, Castro would've had him in his private office asking questions.

General Martinez arranged for my mother to be taken care of until she gave birth. She was picked up in the middle of the night from her tiny apartment in Regla where she lived with her mother, and was taken to a farm on the outskirts of the city.

When I was born, he came by to see me. Told my mother I looked just like his mother, and that she should name me Eugenia. My mother told him she had no intentions of naming me after a woman she didn't even know.

"Her name is Milena. Milena Martinez or Milena Campos?" she asked.

He told her he could never legally recognize me as his daughter because it would ruin his military career.

She yelled and reminded him of the fact that he had been the one to pursue her for weeks at the cabaret, and that later on, when she finally gave in to him, he had not wanted to use any protection. Enraged, she jumped on top of my father. He pushed her off, grabbed her by the neck and punched her face so hard she lost a tooth.

While she was on the floor, he kneeled down next to her and told her that if she ever did go to the authorities, he would have us both killed. He was a powerful man who could make us disappear, and no one would even bother to look. That was the last time she ever saw my father. Two years later he defected in Costa Rica, then we found out he had gone to Miami.

"We would have had the same last name," Kassandra said when I was done with the story. "We could even be sisters, who knows?" On the foot of her bed it said Martinez.

Just then, the doctor came in to check on her. She was released, but the baby had some complications, bacteria in her lungs. She would have to stay another week or so. I was also released with no one picking me up. We were both getting ready to leave the room when one of the nurses walked in with someone following her.

"Surprise," she said, pointing behind her to a black man who was dressed completely in white and held a bunch of pink jasmines in his hands.

Kassandra's face turned pale, a mixture of surprise and terror. The man had to go around my bed to get to hers. He smiled politely at me.

"Hija mia," he said stretching out his hands to her.

Daughter? Kassandra had pretty green eyes and brown reddish hair. Her complexion was fair and gaunt. She had no trace of black in her. People always told me they could tell I had black in me because of my big lips, my flat nose, my not so straight dark hair and my huge butt, which was deemed a sure sign of an African bloodline. But not Kassandra. There was nothing on her face that told of a black father.

"Padrino," she said. "What are you doing here?"

"I come to see my daughter and granddaughter!"

As he hugged her, she looked my way in a panic. She didn't give back the hug, simply stood there licking her lips.

The man in white said something in the Yoruba dialect. It was soon clear to me that he was into Santeria, a combination of Christianity and Yoruba, an ancient people whose occult religion was named after the tribe itself. When a "child of the religion" sees her padrino— her religious godfather— she's supposed to be nervous if she knows she's done something wrong. They are the judges of your life.

In my country, you're either a child of the religion or of the Revolution. Kassandra didn't know whose baby she had had. This was not acceptable in any religion. But in Santeria, it could cost you your life. I knew the vernacular details of the religion by growing up with it all around me. But my mother never really practiced it, and neither did I. We had some general ideas about Catholicism, but the churches were either closed or in such a state of dilapidation that it was dangerous to be in them. My mother had almost forgotten the little her mother had taught her about Jesus Christ. We just believed in God our own way. Either through the saints of Catholicism or their equivalent in Santeria, we were sure that ultimately, the word that really mattered was God's.

"Where is she? I want to see her." Padrino asked the nurse.

"She was just put in an incubator."

"So I can't see her right now?"

"Padrino, she has to stay here a couple of days. You can take me home and her, too," Kassandra said pointing to me.

The man looked puzzled. "Who is she?"

"She's my friend. She's been with me all these days. She has no one picking her up. I thought we could take her home."

"Where do you live, muchachita?"

"La Habana Vieja," I answered.

"That's where we live. We'll go to our house, eat something, then you walk home."

"Thank you."

We rode a very old but well kept Mercedes Benz. Kassandra and I sat in the back while padrino was in the passenger seat and a man with an overextended jaw drove us. I had only ridden a car a few times, never a Mercedes. Kassandra kept her face to the window, and every so often she wiped the tears on her cheeks with the back of her hand. I reached over to touch her leg.

"Back to my life," she said, almost in a whisper. I

could say nothing even though I wanted to take her by the hand and run out of the car. She knew what I was thinking and patted my hand on her thigh.

"You'll be all right," she said very low. "I'm the one that's in trouble."

I thought she was referring to the baby's father and didn't know what kind of trouble she was in.

The section of the city called La Habana Vieja was filled with eighteenth century buildings that were being held up only by the grace of God and hundreds of thousands of two by eight beams. The structural columns had not been touched in at least a century. The paint on some buildings was practically non-existent, and it looked as if the slightest wind would bring down the entire city. I knew these buildings all too well. Tia Susi had lived here all her life. My mother and I used to visit at least once a month. And for the past thirty days, it had been my home.

I didn't say anything in the car ride because chances were that this family knew who my tia was, and they would know who I was. The word in town was that the dancer's daughter was now living either with her aunt or in La Habana with a friend. Nobody knew for sure. My mom had instructed my aunt to do this, so the state wouldn't come after me and send me to work in the sugar cane fields or the literacy camps the Revolution had established for the country folk.

Ironically, one of the reasons my mother had not taken me with her was that she wanted me to finish school. I had not been able to go to school anymore and had had to stay indoors all the time.

Padrino lived in a huge but ancient house in such a state of obliteration that pieces of stucco collected on the floor exposing the skeleton of the structure. The paint on the walls had disappeared in big chunks, leaving only trails of what used to be a well kept home. It stood on crutches as the other buildings, with wooden beams holding it. The conditions inside were the same, but it was clean. The furniture was from Batista's time, and even though I was too young to remember the previous dictator, I had been to other houses where the furniture was still standing in a time warp.

"Bienvenida," Padrino said to me. "You are always welcomed here as long as you're Kassandra's friend."

"Thank you," I said, somewhat skeptical about his conditional politeness.

Kassandra smiled. "And when you're no longer my friend, you may still come here, but you have to pay the fees."

"Kassandra, you talk too much," Padrino said. "That's always going to be your problem."

"Yes, well, I have to tell her the truth, no?"

I stood wondering why she felt she needed to tell me the truth about everything. I didn't think it was my place to say a word. I hoped to have a few minutes by ourselves to ask Kassandra why things felt so tense with her padrino.

"Kassandra is a nice girl, but sometimes she has to bite her tongue," he said as if telling me would make me a part of his disciplining team. "I hope you're not learning all the wrong things from her."

"No, Padrino," Kassandra responded. "I promise I'll teach her to be as good as I am." She winked an eye at me.

The man in white excused himself and walked through a wooden door that had no handle. Kassandra grabbed my hand and pulled me onto the stairs.

"Come on, let me show you where I sleep when I stay here."

"Don't you live here?"

"No, Camacho and I usually stay in a room in La Habana at this little old lady's house. We give her two hundred pesos a month because sometimes we don't want to pay for a cab to bring us back here."

"Camacho is your boyfriend?"

"Yep. He's my Padrino's nephew. I met him at my initiation into the religion. I was very young and fell in love with him."

"Is he here?"

"I don't think so, or he would've come down to see us already. He's really pissed at me, so I don't think I'll see him for a while."

The second floor was held by marble columns that in deep contrast to the rest of the house, were still in pretty good shape. We walked by a couple of rooms with open doors, they were bedrooms with colorful furniture, tables and chairs with kaleidoscopic colors and designs. The farthest room had the door closed.

"Yuk, what's in there?" I asked when we passed by it.

"That's where Eleggua gets his sacrificial lambs," Kassandra answered.

Eleggua was one the most powerful saints of the religion and he liked to drink chicken's blood and have their feet at his altar. When I was seven, we had a neighbor who was a high priestess, and she would tell me if I wasn't a good little girl, Eleggua would have my long curls as a sacrifice. The sacrificial lambs were not real lambs, (real lamb was a rare delicacy) they were pieces of roosters, pigs, goats, and chickens.

We continued into a small hall, which led to narrow stairs into the attic. The walls were bare with old paint peeling from everywhere. There was a canopy bed in the middle of the room which was enveloped by a thick mosquito net, a luxury not everyone had in the island's mosquito riddled summers. The bed had not been slept in for a while, and things looked as if no one had been in there for years. This was Kassandra's room.

"I haven't been in here since I found out I was pregnant."

"How come?"

"We just stay in different places, and lately we've been with Lucia. She takes care of me. She cooks whatever I want to eat. She washes my clothes, and never asks any questions. I had no reason to come back here."

"But isn't this home?"

"This used to be home when I was a little girl. My

mother and I slept in this room and when she went to work, I stayed with my padrino and his wife."

"Did they know?"

"They're the ones that put her to work as soon as she was old enough to do so."

"How old was that?"

"She was fifteen."

"And you started at twelve?"

"And they keep getting younger. The Revolution's thirst for young girls is never ending," she said taking my hand. "Let's get out of here."

We went down a set of stairs that led into the patio. There were wooden altars on every corner of the patio. One had a Chango, the other a Yemaya and in the corner closer to us there was Oludamare, the king of the orishas.

Kassandra crossed herself three times in front of Chango, which meant this was her matron saint, the orisha she was supposedly protected by. She took some stale bread that was in a bowl and dropped to her knees in front of the decorated coconut. The fruit had been given eyes and a mouth, hair and a nose, and it sat on a small wooden chair covered with a large red pillowcase. There were eggs with painted faces surrounding the bowl it sat in, where a bed of centavos had been made to accommodate the machete-flattened bottom. She offered the bread to the saint, prayed in the Yoruba dialect, then crossed herself again.

I had seen people praying to these saints before. They usually danced and whirled around in a demented fashion. Kassandra simply interlaced her fingers placing her chin on them as she closed her eyes. It reminded me of how my mother used to pray before she went on a trip.

An old black woman with a wrinkled face, hair pulled back and dressed completely in white stood at the door of the patio. She also crossed herself as she walked in front of one of the decorated coconuts, but not the same one Kassandra was kneeling in front of.

When Kassandra noticed her, she stood quickly and took a few steps and kneeled next to her. The old woman smiled but continued her prayers without looking sideways. A few minutes went by in silence while the nauseating smell of rotten flesh permeated the courtyard. My stomach suddenly went into painful contortions, and I had to dash up the stairs to what, during the walkthrough with Kassandra, I had narrowly made out to be the bathroom.

Once I was done emptying the already scarce contents of my stomach, I stepped outside the bathroom trying not to inhale too deeply for the putrid odor was pervasive, when I heard a man's voice coming from the first floor. I took a step back into the bathroom and pushed one of the shades to look down.

"That's what I like to see," a man said. "Family sticking with family."

The old woman and Kassandra were both still on their knees while the light-skinned mulatto stood close to them. Kassandra's expression was the same it had been when she first saw her padrino in the hospital; an eerie mix of panic and surprise.

"Camacho, where have you been?" the old woman asked getting up to kiss and hug him.

"Ay, abuela, I'm a busy man. I have businesses to attend to. I can't be coming here all the time."

"I know you can't come here all the time," she responded. "Pero mi hijo, I haven't seen you in over three months."

"I know I know..."

"Ochun hasn't seen you in a while either, Camacho. You cannot abandon your religion like that."

"My religion's captain is the American dollar, abuela."

"Don't speak like that in front of Ochun."

I smiled at the old belief that saints could hear you. Camacho hugged his grandmother without taking his eyes off Kassandra.

"Where's the baby?" he asked her.

"In the hospital."

"Does it look like me or the Yuma you fucked?" He circled her like a hunting dog does to his soon to be prey.

"This might not be the best place to talk about that, Camacho," she said, lowering her head submissively.

"This is as good a place as the streets of La Habana where you told me it might not be mine."

"Might not be yours?" the old woman asked confused.

"She had a white Yuma at the same time she was with me, and now she doesn't even know who the father is."

The old woman looked at Kassandra, then back at her grandson. "You young people are all crazy. In my time, no one had babies without being married."

"Yeah well, the women back then respected their men, abuela."

"And men respected their women," Kassandra said.

"You're saying I didn't respect you?" Camacho's voice was louder now, angrier, and his eyes glowed furiously. Suddenly, he took a few steps toward her and grabbed the back of her neck pushing her face down to the floor.

Kassandra didn't scream. She took a deep breath resisting, but not fighting back. The old woman let out two short cries. "What are you doing, Camacho?" she yelled.

He looked up, held on to Kassandra's neck for a second longer, then let go but not before shoving her face onto the rough floor.

"That is not the way I taught you to treat women! What is wrong with you?" the old woman said running toward Kassandra who was trying to get back up. I stood behind the bathroom door. Fear cemented my feet. I felt complete repulsion for this man and instinctively knew he was dangerous. Kassandra's overwhelming fear of staying in La Habana was no longer so puzzling.

"Camacho, get the hell out of here!" the old lady yelled. "Get out before I get your uncle to kick you out."

"Ay, abuela, I'm going I'm going. But you don't scare me with my uncle, he won't do anything for a whore."

"Get out of my house!"

"I'll see you around el malecon," he said to Kassandra and walked out.

I stepped out of the bathroom and ran down the steps. Kassandra was nervous but did not cry. On her face was the resignation that is common in the Cuban people, the knowing that no matter how much they want change, change is nowhere to be found.

"Ay mijita," said the old woman holding on to Kassandra. "How I wish that grandson of mine and you had never met."

"Are you okay?" I asked when I got to the bottom of the stairs.

"You talk to your padrino, you hear me," the old woman ordered. "He'll put Camacho in check. He's always had to be that boy's father and mother. He's the only man Camacho respects. You tell him what he's done to you."

"Okay, abuela," Kassandra said looking down.

"I have to lie in bed. My heart can't take these scenes anymore; I think I'm going to die." The old woman stood and headed up the stairs.

"She's been dying for the last twenty years," Kassandra whispered. "We should go."

"But aren't you going to say something?"

"To whom?"

"Your padrino!"

"My padrino loves me, but I'm not his blood so he won't do anything about it."

"What's wrong is wrong; he has to do something

about it."

"What do you know, huh? You've known us a total of five minutes."

"You have to do something about what just happened."

"Running to my padrino is definitely not the answer. Trust me. Right now, we just need to get out of here."

I followed her as we left the house without saying goodbye to anyone. Two blocks down, with the help of two men already hanging on, we jumped onto the back of a bus so cramped with people that inside you could not tell whose arm belonged to whose face.

At a major intersection, we jumped off saying thank you to the two guys who had helped us hang on. We had no money for a cab, so we had a choice. We either walked to Centro Habana or we hitched a ride from a tourist.

"Male tourists," Kassandra explained, "love to help out young girls in distress. Who knows, we might even be able to make some money off of them."

The streets were filled with pedestrians and bicycles, few cars and buses, all models from the fifties. The scent of rotting wood from the rundown buildings mixed in with excrement from the pigs and chickens that people kept in their bathtubs permeated the busy boulevard, and stuck to your clothes and skin.

A thirty-something-year old yellow Pontiac stopped to pick us up. It was driven by an old man who knew Kassandra and Camacho's family. She made small talk with him for the short ride. When he dropped us off at

La Quinta Avenida, Kassandra blew a kiss his way.

"Yuk," she said smelling her underarm as we walked. "With this funky smell we're never going to get a client. Let's go shower at your house."

"Are you crazy? I can't just show up with you at my aunt's house."

"Just tell her I was with you in the hospital, and I'm on my way back to the country. Tell her I'm from Matanzas."

"She doesn't care where you're from. I can't bring a stranger into her house. Plus she's back in La vieja. Why don't we go to your place here?"

"Camacho is probably there waiting to send me back to the hospital."

"You think he'll just sit around all day waiting for you?"

"You might be right; he has to attend to his other jineteras. We'll watch from the corner until he steps out, go in, shower, change, and take off. I have a hundred dollars in one of my boots."

"In one of your boots?"

"My working boots. In the heel. You break it off and then glue it back on. It was the only place I knew Camacho wouldn't think of." She stopped, deep in thought, then with audacious lucidity, continued with her improvised plan.

"I think the two of us together stick out more than if we're by ourselves. You're gonna have to wait in the corner while I go inside."

"You're quite the detective, huh?" I said trying to infuse the situation with some well needed humor. It didn't work.

"My mother loved American movies, too. She used to retell the stories until I fell asleep. You learn a lot from the Americans because they are smart people. That's why I want Kristen to grow up there."

"Kristen? Is that her name?"

"Do you like it? A client told me that was his daughter's name and that I looked like her."

"I like it," I said. "And it starts with a k, like yours, right?"

Kassandra gave me a full-of-love smile, a gesture I had not yet seen in her. We separated and took our posts. People walked by without noticing us. I could see Kassandra's red hair from behind the pole of the streetlight that didn't work. An hour went by. My feet were tired, my stomach growled and I peeked out from behind the pole. She signaled for me to hide. Just then, the door we were watching opened up and out came Camacho fixing the collar on his shirt.

He took a couple of steps, stopped, looked both ways deciding which he would take, and started walking in my direction. I stuck my spine against the pole and I could feel the beads of sweat being absorbed by the clothes I wore. Then I realized that if he saw me hiding behind the pole, he would suspect something. So I started to walk quickly toward him. As he passed me, he made an inappropriate comment about my behind, but I just smiled nervously and kept walking, not daring to glance in his direction.

When he had turned the corner up the street, Kassandra was already approaching the door to the apartment. I crossed the intersection and followed her in. The downstairs room was tiny, windowless, with a full-size bed, a nightstand and a bathroom, which also served as a closet. There were piles of clothes in each of the four corners. It smelled of cigarettes and booze.

"I know it's nasty in here, but we'll be gone soon. I'll shower first and while you shower, I'll pick up some of my things."

I stepped over what looked like a spilled drink that had sat there too long. The small room had the bare necessities; no luxuries or pictures anywhere.

"I wonder why Lucia has not come in to clean," Kassandra said, looking in the closet/bathroom. "She usually does once a week but he probably hasn't paid her. Where the hell are my boots?"

"Maybe he told her not to," I said, picking up some of the clothes that served as the only decorations, to help her look for the boots.

"Maybe he was waiting for me to come home to do it. You can just leave those. I don't think I'll take them with me."

I threw the clothes in a corner already occupied by some more rags. "Isn't he going to know you were here?"

"Yes." She continued to ruffle through piles of clothes and shoes.

"You don't care?"

"All I care about is getting my daughter and getting out of here."

"You mean La Habana?"

"I mean the island. I have someone that will take

Kristen and me to Miami on a boat. He's asking for five thousand dollars. If I work really hard for a couple of weeks, I think I could do it. The only problem is Camacho. He runs a lot of the jineteras on el malecon. I could find clients somewhere else, but..."

"But..." I echoed.

"But it would be easier to make more money if there's two of us," she said ceasing the search for a moment to look up at me, then continued. "I have no idea where my boots are. Shit!"

I watched her while she searched. I knew that most girls my age had done some sexual favor with a tourist for dollars. But most of the stories I had heard never included full penetration. The girls just did other things. I knew my mother would have been disappointed. But I was alone and like my Tia said, I had to fend for myself.

"How is it going to be easier if there's two of us?" I asked.

"What man doesn't want to see two young girls fuck each other?"

"Are you serious?"

She nodded. "We'll go to Havana Club where a lot of tourists go. I'll go in first. You wait for me outside because we don't want to spend money in paying for two entrances. I'll find a client in there, and I'll make him come out to get you. We'll spend some time with him and then we go to his hotel. It's easier than you think."

"I've only had sex a few times, Kassandra."

"Perfect. At least your first won't be a client."

"But..."

"Listen, the first time is the hardest. If you really think you can't do it, then let me know now, and I'll give you some cab fare back to your aunt's house."

I wanted to be tough, independent, determined like her. I wanted to leave the island and make a life for myself in the U.S., like my mother had wanted. But I wasn't sure I could do this.

"I don't want to go back there."

"Then come on. We'll do this together, and I'll help you. You'll see that after a couple of times, it's no big deal," she said, stepping into the dirty bathtub.

My mother's voice swirled in my head. It was distant, almost inaudible. Since she left, I had heard it clear and steady. If I closed my eyes I could see her smile anytime. Now, I pressed my eyelids together tight, and still could not picture her clearly.

"There's no hot water!" Kassandra yelled from the tiny bathroom.

I sat in a corner of the bed crying. It was the first time since my mother's departure that I felt truly alone. Even though it had been explained to me that she had probably drowned, the fact that her body was never found still gave me hope.

I suppose in a subconscious attempt at denial, I had imagined she had survived and was in an American prison where she could not understand anything. Soon, the Cuban government would find out she was alive, and they would send me to her.

The reality of what my life was going to be without her hit me, and I could do nothing more than cry.

Kassandra kept yelling about the water being cold. I heard the shower shut off. With the back of my hand, I wiped the tears before she saw them. She stepped out of the shower dripping. Her stomach and breasts were still swollen, but other than that, she didn't look like she had just had a baby. She had a curvy thin body with a waist so small that once the swelling went down, you could enclose it in both hands.

"Your turn," Kassandra announced drying her self. "The water's cold but at least it's running. So hurry!"

I took off my clothes and stepped into the tub. There was a thick rim of dirt all around the middle of it and the corners were filled with hair. I took a deep breath and grabbed the thin bar of cheap European soap. I could hear Kassandra still ruffling through clothes looking for the boots.

"My fucking boots are not here!" she yelled. I turned the water off and immediately received a wet towel over the shower curtain.

"I can't find another towel. Hope you don't mind."

"It's fine," I said drying myself. I wrapped the towel around my body and pushed the curtain to the side. Kassandra was still naked.

"I wore them two days before I went to the hospital, came here, changed. Yes, I left them here. They have to be here."

"I'll help you look."

"Unless that son of a bitch brought someone here and gave them to her."

"He'd do that?"

"There aren't many things Camacho wouldn't do,

Milena."

"You still think he loved you?"

She paused for a moment. "I'd like to believe he did."

She said little and I had so much to say. I wanted to tell her I was still not sure I could go through with her proposition. But she threw some of her clothes my way and told me to put them on. Then she sat me down on the toilet and began putting make-up on. She did the same to her face. In less than a half-hour we were ready. She scrounged some of the loose change around the room, and we walked out into the early evening. I felt awkward in clothes that were too tight and heels that were half a size too big for me.

Kassandra hailed a cab and told the driver that we did not have any money, but that we were on our way to meet some rich extranjeros and there would be a twenty dollar tip for him. The driver, an old man without front teeth, smiled and told us to get in.

Havana Club, the most popular discoteca on the island, was in an old cigar warehouse in Miramar that had been bought by an investor. We did exactly as Kassandra had planned. It wasn't long before she came out to get me. She already had fifty dollars in her hand.

"How did you make that money so quick?" I asked her as she dragged me inside.

"I bumped into one of my favorite clients. He's English, not American, but he's very nice and very rich."

The man was sitting alone at a table with a

champagne bottle resting in an ice bucket. The waitress was flirting with him. Kassandra gave her a dismissive look, and the girl disappeared into the mass of people.

I was introduced as her friend, no name was mentioned, and he didn't ask. He seemed smitten with Kassandra, perhaps the red hair and sultry green eyes or her witty disposition. Whatever it was, he could not take his eyes or hands off her. I watched her work him. She laughed, kissed him, caressed his thick black hair. She kept his champagne glass filled all the time while she took small sips of hers.

At one point she stood, pulled my hands up to her hips and lifted me slowly from the leathery seats. The she started dancing slowly with me, making sure her eyes were on the client and her hands were all over me. Because I had been sitting, watching her and slowly sipping my champagne most of the night, when I stood, the floor moved under my feet. I held tightly onto her tiny waist for balance. She pushed the back of my neck into her shoulder. Her neck was supple and smelled like vanilla, a splash she had offered in her bathroom, but I had declined claiming sweet perfumes weren't my thing. Now the scent, or the combination of it with champagne, made me want her.

"Okay, it's time," she whispered minutes later. "Let's get in the taxi and go to his hotel."

I wanted to tell her I didn't think I could walk outside. I felt as if someone was running laps around in my head. As soon as she stepped away from me, she realized I could not follow her. She took my hand firmly and pulled me back down to the high backed booth. My head fell into my hands between my knees. I could hear Kassandra telling me to breathe deeply. But my stomach was in my throat, and breathing was difficult. She lifted my head with one hand and stuck the other in the ice bucket. The ice water on my neck and face was surprisingly pleasant. She smiled.

"You're gonna be okay; it's good champagne. Let's get out of here." She wet my lips with an ice cube, wiped my face, and shook me to a stand up position. I felt just a tinge better. The English guy had to be carried out by a bouncer. Outside, the cabdriver smiled as he opened the door for us while the bouncer placed the English guy by a window, in case he needed to vomit.

Kassandra and I sat close together; she kept blowing air on my neck and face. "You need to look a little more alive. We can't walk into the hotel with you looking like this."

She gave the driver instructions as she reached into her bra to take out a few bills and give him one.

"That was the waitress's tip," she whispered. "She had already made her money with him. She didn't even know he had this for her."

"How did you take it?"

"He told me to give it to her. She didn't deserve it. She didn't even come around once you and I got there."

The English guy made a strange sound with his throat. We moved closer to our window to give him plenty of space. He folded in half preparing to release most of his dinner so Kassandra made the driver stop the cab. She got out and pulled the English man's body out. He tried to say something, instead out came the champagne and dinner.

"There there, James" she said patting his back. "You'll feel better now."

In the hotel, the concierge was very pleasant. He recognized Kassandra and she gave him some dollars to let us in the room with James. Cubans were not allowed in the hotels of the city, neither as patrons nor visitors, but in some places, money could take care of that. I was feeling less drunk but somewhat nauseated. Kassandra and I each took one of the English guy's arms, wrapped it around our shoulders and headed toward the elevator with him. The concierge smiled at her. He was a short young man with a thin smile. Even in my drunkenness, I could tell right away he liked her.

"Many of the guys that work in the hotels like me because I give them money. Plus, they know what I am, and some think if they're nice to me, they can get some free of charge. Nobody gets any free of charge, you hear me?" Everything from now on was going to be a lesson in the business, she said.

"Unless you have a chulo. And if you do, you're crazy. Look at what happened to me."

Lesson number one: no chulos, no free sex. The elevator door opened up, and we pulled the English guy out. He could barely stand. Kassandra stuck her hand in his pockets looking for the key. She found his wallet. Inside, there were still some dollar bills, his identification papers and the plastic room key.

"Lesson number two," she said. "Take everything you can. You might not get another chance." She stuck the money in between her breasts and slid the key into the door.

I had been to some hotel rooms with my mother when she traveled in Cuba. But this was no ordinary room. There was a room before another room, I later learned it was called a living room, and a meeting room. The bedroom had a one-armed antique chair sitting in front of the window, which faced the huge bed. There was a large bathroom with a shower and a hot tub that could fit five.

Kassandra pointed to the bed. We dropped the English guy on it like we were carrying a sack of rocks but he didn't flinch.

"Your first night working and you don't even have to. This guy's not waking up until morning," she said. I smiled. "You must be a daughter of Yemaya, did you know she's the matron saint of prostitutes?"

"I did not know that," I said. "But a santera once told my mother she's my saint."

"She read your caracoles?"

"No, I've never had that done. She just looked at me and said I was a daughter of La Virgen de Regla. Maybe because I'm from there?"

Almost everyone my mother and I came across who practiced the religion told us I had to be a daughter of Yemaya, because of my long hair and my not so aquiline features such as my flat nose. Not sure why, but for this, I was supposed to be very lucky. I believed it. But then I lost my mother. And I assumed I wasn't really a "daughter" of the popular lucky saint.

"Puf, I'm tired," Kassandra said dropping into the one armed long chair. "Let's get a good night sleep because we're gonna have to work in the morning. That's the way he likes it. Bright and early."

I was sitting on the edge of the bed where the English guy's body lay splattered in the middle. I pushed his body to the other side and lay down. Out the window, the sun was coming up, and the warm rays of light touched my face slightly. My head spun a few more times before I finally fell asleep.

CHAPTER TWO

When I woke up, I had an unfamiliar pounding headache accompanied by the same dreadful nausea. I ran to the bathroom. After throwing up until my cheeks hurt, I washed my face and mouth. The English guy was still out.

Kassandra sat on the edge of the chair she had slept on, her red mane over half a face that showed signs of a late night. She put one finger over her lips signaling silence, grabbed my hand and took me back into the bathroom.

"He's gonna get up soon," she whispered. "I'm going to order some room service," she looked around, "and a maid to clean up this mess. This will be the easiest money you'll ever make, you'll see."

"What do you want me to do?"

"Just follow my lead and be calm. He's really easy to get off. Ten minutes and he's done, especially with the two of us."

"Okay," I said. We stepped out to find the English guy also trying to recuperate. He was holding his head in his hands over the edge of the bed.

"Hi, James, how you feeling this beautiful

morning?" Kassandra said jumping on the bed.

"I have a bloody headache."

"I'll make you better in no time," she said maneuvering his weak body to land on top of it. She started taking his clothes off. I was stuck to the floor, paralyzed until she ordered me to get on the bed with her.

We took the rest of his clothes off and Kassandra grabbed his flaccid penis. She tried to sit on it. I sat half in shock, half excited next to them. I liked the way she took control of the situation, and so did James. She continued to stroke his testicles while moving up and down on him. She looked at me and smiled as if to say you're doing a good job. I simply touched his chest and watched her.

"Oh, James, you're so good," Kassandra moaned. I could tell it was fake by the way she looked at me and tried to hide her smile. James moaned as well. Suddenly, he stopped and looked at me.

"Suck it," he said. "I want you to suck it when I come."

"I'll suck it, papi," Kassandra said. "I know how you like it when you're coming."

"Nah, I want her to do it. I want her to suck it, now." He pushed Kassandra off, pulled my head to his penis and stuck it in my mouth. I felt the veins expand and the penis getting harder. Then, a burst of warm thick liquid in my mouth as he pushed my face even harder while he moaned. I wanted to pull away and spit out everything. But he had a strong hold on my hair and kept my face from moving. I could hardly breathe and had to swallow a gulp of air along with some semen. He finally released my head as I pulled away disgusted and ready to throw up again.

"That's my papi," cheered Kassandra lightly clapping her hands. She reached for a pack of cigarettes on the bedside table, lit one and gave it to him. I spit the rest of the semen onto the pillow and wiped my face with the sheets. James was almost out again, the cigarette hanging from the corner of his mouth. There was a knock on the door and Kassandra jumped to put on a robe.

It was room service. "I need money for tip," Kassandra said to James. He reached lethargically for his wallet, but the cigarette rolled over his shoulder onto the bed. He tried to jump up on one elbow to get it. Kassandra reached for the wallet on the bedside table.

"I'll get it," she said, handing the man a couple of dollars.

James managed to retrieve the cigarette, but not before it opened a big hole in the sheet and mattress. He then lay back down and crunched a couple of pillows under his head as he inhaled a long drag. With his right hand he caressed my thigh.

"I like you a lot," he said. "You and Kassie make a great team."

"It's all about the right customer, I told her," Kassandra said preparing a plate. "I told her she was lucky to have you as her first customer."

"Am I really your first customer?"

I nodded.

"Didn't she do well?" Kassandra said, bringing the plate to the bed.

"She certainly did," he said, smiling.

I forced a smile trying to be like Kassandra. James took the back of my head and pushed my face down forcing my lips on his. The taste of cigarettes and alcohol was sickening, but I held my breath. I managed to retrieve my head saying I needed to use the bathroom. Kassandra and James started to eat.

In the bathroom, I looked in the mirror to see a brand new person whose eyes I did not recognize. My skin, cracking at the corners of my mouth, seemed older, used and dirty.

I cried. The door to the bathroom opened and Kassandra stood in the middle of it, naked.

"Are you okay?" she asked. She held some fruit in her hand and offered it to me. I shook my head. My stomach continued to churn and the last thing I wanted to do was put anything in it.

"Eat something; you'll feel better."

"I can't," I said. "I really don't feel so good."

"The worst part is over and we're three hundred dollars richer."

I took a deep breath, nodded in acceptance. "I cried the first time too," she said coming closer. "I told you it gets easier each time, and then you'll wonder why you ever cried at all."

"I'm crying for my mother; she would never approve of what I'm doing."

"She isn't here anymore, and you have to find a way to survive. What are you going to do? Go back to your aunt's to get sick with rotten food and to sleep on the cot?"

I shook my head.

"Then tough it out," she continued. "Come out with me; let's get some food so we can get going. We have to find more clients for tonight."

"Okay," I said meagerly, and followed her outside. James was getting dressed with a new cigarette hanging from his lips.

"Is there any trouble?" he asked.

"Nope, she just feels a little woozy still from the champagne," Kassandra responded.

"You should eat something," he said. "I have some business partners coming in tonight. Are you girls available?"

Kassandra's eyes opened wide. "Of course we're available." She looked at me and winked an eye. I forced a smile and a nod at the same time.

"The problem is we have nothing nice to wear if we go out," she said biting into a small red fruit I later learned was a strawberry.

"That's not a problem," James said reaching for his wallet. Kassandra ran to jump on him.

"Now, now, you know I'm an old man. Don't abuse me." He managed to say trying to hang on to the cigarette, the wallet and Kassandra's thin body.

"You're not old," she said taking his face in her hands. "You are the best!" She kissed his face repeatedly and rubbed her body on his. I started putting my shoes on while the "love scene" took place.

"When we come back, I'm gonna suck it like you

like it, papi," Kassandra said gathering her clothes.

"Your friend there did a pretty good job. Maybe today we switch again."

"You don't like me anymore? Now you like my friend?"

"I like you both."

"You know my feelings get hurt easily," she said with a wink.

She was obviously feigning jealousy because I knew she could care less about who he liked best. I started to understand that Kassandra's touch with men had everything to do with the way she made them feel when they were with her. She made sure they felt special and important, and that even if the sex was no good, they felt like champions afterwards.

James took us to a store to buy clothes. He picked out what he wanted us to wear and then took us back to the hotel. I was hungry and exhausted and my headache had not gone away. We ordered some room service again and modeled the clothes for him. Then he wanted sex again. I took a long shower claiming it would make my headache go away.

When I was done, James had already left. Kassandra was sitting on the bed counting cash.

"He didn't even realize I took the hundred dollars last night."

"What did you tell him?"

"Nothing. I told him he had to pay us before he left, and he looked in his wallet. He thought about it for a moment but then went to the safe right there," she pointed to a watercolor of Varadero, "and took out another two hundred."

"So we have five hundred dollars?

"In one night. Have you ever made so much money so easily?"

I had given haircuts to my friends and occasionally done a manicure to an old neighbor for a peso or two, but that was the extent of my working experience. When the government had asked my mother to send me to work in the schools in the fields, she got one of her friend doctors to sign a paper stating I could not due to a severe asthmatic condition. So while the rest of the girls my age went off to the countryside to plow the fields and teach the guajiros to read, I stayed in Regla and went to regular school.

She counted two hundred dollars from the pile on the bed and handed it to me.

"I don't know what to do with this," I said looking at the bills in my hand.

"What do you mean you don't know what to do with it?"

"Where do I put it?"

"Here, give it to me. I'll keep it with my money. When we part ways, I'll give it to you."

"When we part? Where are you going?"

"Do you not listen to anything I say?"

I shrugged.

"As soon as I can get five thousand dollars, I'm going to Miami with my daughter."

"I want to go with you."

"You need five grand to pay for the boat ride."

"I won't make that on my own."

"No, you won't. I was thinking when you went out that we could do this together and make the money really fast. But none of this crying bullshit in a client's bathroom. You hear me?"

I didn't answer. For a moment I thought I was looking at a total stranger. But I still felt the need to stay with her, to protect her, to help her and Kristen. Perhaps then my mother would forgive me. Even if I had done something she could not be proud of, at the end, it was also ultimately for the good of others. Getting out of Cuba had been her deepest wish, for me to learn the American ways was what she wanted more than anything in the world, what she had died for. I needed to believe Kassandra had the same dream for her daughter and my helping her was the best way to somewhat validate my mother's death.

"I know it was your first time, and I know he grosses you out. But if you're serious about this, you're gonna have to be tougher."

"I might need some time," I said holding back another tear.

"We don't have that luxury, Milena. At least I don't. I need this money within a week, two at the most. Camacho is not going to give up; he's gonna find me."

"So let's go to the police. They have to protect you," I said.

Her expression suddenly softened and I saw a young girl with a lot of pain in her eyes, much like mine had been hours before in front of that same mirror.

"What world do you come from?" she asked.

"What do you mean?"

"I mean how could you be so naïve when you grew up in the heart of this city?"

"I don't think I'm naïve for thinking the police will protect you from this guy. Our country is not in such bad shape."

"Oh that's right, I forgot your mother must have taught you what she believed, which was that communism works because justice is established."

"My mother was not a communist. She didn't like the system any more than you and I do. But she thought some things about it worked."

"Like what?"

"Like everyone is equal, and..." she didn't let me finish.

"You know what the cops are gonna do when we go to them? Go tell Camacho exactly where to find me, so he can give them a couple of dollars each. That's how it works."

I could tell by now when she was lying. She wasn't lying this time. She had tears in her eyes again, and so did I.

"Stop it already!" She said pretending to be mad at me. "I'm not going to the police. I'll never see my daughter again."

I took her hands in mine and said, "You'll see her again. Tomorrow we'll go see her."

Her face changed and I saw the pretty green eyes sparkle.

"So tonight we work!" I said, clasping my hands

for reassurance. "We make another five hundred and tomorrow we go see Kristen, and in a week we'll have the money to get the fuck outta here."

I imitated her gestures trying to be funny. I wasn't used to cursing, and when I did, it didn't sound as natural as when she did. She smiled.

"If James comes back, we don't want to fuck him again until tonight."

"That's good because he does gross me out. You?" I asked, admiring the way she went from emotional to businesslike in a split second.

"I've been doing this a while, and I know my customers already, and they still gross me out. But I gotta do it. With James it's easier than with others. He tries to get as much as possible for the money he pays, but he likes to spend time with me. So if we're not here, and we're at a bar somewhere having some drinks, he'll join us. We'll come back to the room, shower, and get ready to pick up his business partners from the airport."

"How many business partners?"

"One or two, maybe three if we're lucky."

"If you take James and I get one, what happens to the other two?"

"You wanna do two in one night?"

"Are you serious?"

"You make double the money."

"I think I'll stick with one for now."

"I know a girl. We can even pay her less money and keep the difference."

"That would be cheating her."

"Yeah, and?"

"How can you do that to a friend?"

She exhaled. "I said I knew her, I didn't say she was my friend and even if she was, she would do it to me."

"What makes me think you wouldn't do that to me?" My mother always told me that whatever someone does to a friend, they would do it to you.

"Because until now all I've done is help you survive, not cheat you."

"I could've survived on my own."

"Not in this business."

"Maybe I wouldn't have gotten into this business at all?"

"What would you have done? Go to work for a hundred pesos a month?"

"Maybe," I said, knowing one couldn't survive on a salary like that when basic necessities could only be bought with dollars.

"Please! You wouldn't last in a factory for a day. Your destiny was to meet me so you can make your mother's dream come true and go to Miami."

"Pa' Miami nos vamos," I said imitating Castro, trying to shake off the feeling that I didn't belong in this life by poking fun at the regime. The one thing you learned fast in Cuba is that when things were bad, you made fun of Fidel. Lately, the citizens had tired of his useless speeches that said nothing and promised changes that never happened. When I was born, people were still afraid to voice their opinion. But now, no one cared anymore. The sense of right and wrong had become jaded in most Cubans; the American dollar, the crack of the Cuban people.

She laughed at my stupid joke and hugged me tight. It was the first time she showed me any real affection. And I welcomed it. Then abruptly, she released me, as if not wanting to let me know how much she really cared.

That night, there was an old but cared for limo waiting for us outside the hotel. We waited about fifteen minutes for James. When he finally appeared, he stuck his head in the window, said he needed to do something and for us to go on without him, that he would meet us at Havana Club.

Kassandra said he had never done that before, but it didn't matter as long as we had clients. The limo drove away with instructions to stay with us the entire night. Kassandra opened the bottle of rum sitting in ice, made two drinks and prepared the glasses for another two. She handed one to me.

"Listen," she said, leaning back into the polished leather, "the more time we spend with them the more they have to pay us. So if they want to go first to the hotel, we say no. We have instructions from James, and that's what we're sticking to because sometimes they want to fuck first."

"Then?"

"We go eat. Anywhere. We go to a nice expensive

restaurant for tourists only. They can afford it, and it's the only way you and I will ever get in one."

"And then?"

"We go to the club. We spend the entire night with them, we show them a good time. A night like that is anywhere from two to five hundred dollars. If you fuck them first, they leave with another jinetera from the club and you won't even get paid. Use your head."

"Got it," I said, looking at the people riding bikes on the streets. The truth was that I didn't feel like I had such a good head on me. I had made a friend who had taught me how to become a prostitute. Now on my way to meet two more new clients, the guilt was riding over me like a dark cloud.

"You're going to feel guilty for not feeling guilty for the rest of your life."

"How do you what I'm thinking?"

"I was there," she said with an air of knowing everything. "A long time ago, but I was there once. You think if this is not right, why do I keep doing it? But you can't stop because you learn nothing else but the hustle of the street." She took a long sip of her drink. "I want to learn other things, like computers or maybe x-rays or something. I want Kristen to go to school in a country where no one knows what her mother has done."

"You don't have to be ashamed."

"I told you, you never stop feeling guilty about not feeling guilty," she said, smiling and sipping at the same time.

Within minutes, we were at Jose Marti

International Airport, which was nothing more than a couple of warehouses strung together, and the huge empty space that was the runway. The driver gave some dollars to the guard at the gate and they let the limo in. After a few turns, we found ourselves in front of a small plane and two men in suits descended the narrow stairs. Our driver got out of the car to open the backdoor for them. Kassandra and I moved closer together.

Two fair-skinned middle-aged men sat in the car. They said hi instead of hello, a clear sign they were Americans. One was maybe forty and the other forty-five. Kassandra immediately went for the older one.

"What's your name?" she asked, a thick accented English. He answered, Kevin, his friend was John.

John was tall, plain and lanky. He tried to start a conversation in Spanish. "Tu ser mucho bonita."

"Thank you." I answered in English so he could stop his atrocities with my language.

"Oh, you speak English, thank god."

"Only little bit."

"But you understand, so that's good for me. "

"You hablas English to me. I hablo Spanish to you."

"Okay, yo hablar solo español con tu. Tu ser bonita brunette." I had no idea what the last word meant. I looked at Kassandra and she told me.

"Ah, don't worry," he said, "we'll figure it out." And he squeezed my shoulders.

He wasn't the nicest looking man, but he was funny and somewhat pleasant. He opened the door for me, helped me out of the car, asked if I felt okay. He sensed my discomfort and tried his best to appease me. He was a gentleman the entire night--as much as any man could be to a prostitute he's planning to have sex with-- and that was the best type of client, Kassandra said.

James never showed up at the club. On our way back to the hotel with the two Yumas, Kevin asked John if James had had the rooms taken care of. I wasn't sure why James had to be responsible for their rooms but said nothing.

"What's going on?" Kevin asked Kassandra. "Have you ever done this with James?"

"No, he's never given me up to some friends. We've gone out with some of his partners before, but I've always ended up with him. It doesn't matter though; as long as you pay in dollars."

John moved closer to me. I could smell the alcohol and cigarettes in his breath.

"Tu conmigo brunette."

"Yes, yes."

Kassandra grabbed my hand, put something in it and closed it. It felt like plastic. A condom.

John, in his drunkenness, smiled happily. "I have some of those, too."

"Que?"

"Yo tener condoms."

"Good," Kassandra jumped in. "Now you both have some."

"I'm not wearing that shit," Kevin slurred.

"Then no Cuban pussy for you!" Kassandra said, laughing. John and I laughed as well.

"I hate condoms," Kevin said. He started to make two more drinks, but Kassandra stopped him saying we didn't want to drink anymore. We needed to sober up a bit to fuck their brains out. They liked that. Once in the suite with two bedrooms, Kassandra pushed me into the bathroom.

"I'm going to be right through that door if you need me. I know this is your real first time, but I think you can do it on your own. Just be calm and let him do whatever he wants. Do you like him a little bit? I think you do. If you like him a little you can enjoy it; it's no big deal!"

"Okay," I said. My throat was dry. I followed her outside.

"They're too drunk to do anything crazy," she whispered. "I think they might last five minutes each, if that."

"Are you guys ready?" she asked facing them cheerfully.

"We want you girls to dance together," Kevin announced. He lay on the bed without his jacket and tie.

Kassandra rolled her eyes. She grabbed my hips and turned me to her. She started to undress me, and put my hand on her dress signaling for me to do the same.

"Don't worry," she whispered into my ear. "Better me than a strange girl, right?"

I had been with a man before; a neighbor that used to travel and bring gifts from all kinds of places. He worked on a cruise line and made a lot of money at his young age of nineteen. But I had never even thought of being with a woman until I met Kassandra.

When she had all our clothes off, Kevin stood and said he needed to use the bathroom. John was blissfully asleep on the couch. I was trying to wake him up when Kevin came out of the bathroom with a tiny white bag in his hand.

"Give him some of this," he said to Kassandra. "He'll be up in no time."

"I don't know if he can even do any. He's out," she said.

"Here, you do some then."

She took the bag and stuck her pinky nail in it. She took the tip of her finger to her nose and inhaled deeply. The white powder disappeared into her. She did the same to the other nostril. I watched her, naked, doing drugs in the wee hours of the morning, with smeared make up on her face, and realized how much I liked her daring personality although I was still unsure about this risky adventure with her.

"You want some?" Kevin asked me.

"No."

"Come on. You've been Miss Goody Two Shoes all night. Take a bump!"

"She's never done it before, Kevin. Leave her alone," Kassandra demanded.

"What kind of whore in Havana has never done coke?"

"Come on," Kassandra said pulling his arm. "Let's go to our room. I feel great!"

"Yeah, let's go. These two are boring."

They disappeared into the connecting door. John's head was over the arm of the couch. He tried to wake up, but was too drunk. I took a small cup, filled it with water and splashed it on his face. Kassandra had warned me all night that if they got too drunk and there was no sex, we might not get paid.

John started coming to. He looked around the room like a lost puppy. Then his eyes focused on me. He smiled. I led him to the bed and undressed him. His penis was somewhat hard but not sufficient to have sex. I bent down to perform oral sex. As his penis began to get harder, I put the condom on and sat on top of him. Nothing, the hardness immediately went away. Then I got on all fours on the bed and rubbed my back into him. I started to feel it get harder again and then penetrating me.

Kassandra had been right. It felt like nothing. Maybe it was the alcohol, maybe the fact that I needed the money, maybe that he was so drunk. But it felt like my insides were numb. I might have counted five strokes before he moaned and fell over to the side of the bed.

"That was great!" He barely said followed by a deep snore. I couldn't believe someone could fall asleep so fast. I went to the bathroom to clean up. Then I lay on the couch and watched him sleep. Within a few minutes, I fell asleep myself.

It must have been an hour later when Kassandra woke me up. She was in an agitated state and hurried me to put my clothes on.

"What's wrong?" I asked her.

"Nothing, we gotta go. Did you get your money?"

"No, he fell asleep."

"I told you money up front!" She yelled. "Get dressed," she said. "I'll get the money from his wallet."

While I put on my clothes, she searched the pockets in John's pants. She found the wallet, took out all the cash that was in it, and stuck it somewhere in her dress. I was half dressed with my shoes in my hands when Kevin burst into the room.

"You fucking puta! Gimme my money!" he screamed like a madman as he lunged forward to grab Kassandra's neck. Kassandra let out a short cry and they both fell to the floor. Kevin was on top of her trying to strangle her. I reacted and quickly jumped on his back. He was so strong that he easily lifted my entire body and threw me on the bed on top of John who didn't even flinch, but simply rolled over to the other side.

I stood again. Kevin was now slapping her. Kassandra did not stop fighting. He held her throat with one hand and slapped and punched her face with the other. I tried to get him off her to no avail. He had the strength of three men. He grabbed my arm and pushed me down to the floor next to her. He let go of her for a split second to slap me only to quickly retrieve her neck and continued to punch her thin body. I managed to stand and looked around the room for something to hit him with. The closest thing was the bulky lamp on the bedside table. I pulled it from the wall and hit him over the head with it. His body fell heavily unconscious next to Kassandra who desperately tried to recover her breath. On the bed, John was slowly coming to. He opened his eyes slowly and scratched his head, and as he sat up, he looked around at the mess in the room. When he found Kevin's body lying down next to the bed, he got up with a jump.

"What the....?"

"He hit her, John," I said hovering over my friend. "I couldn't let him hurt her."

He looked down at Kassandra who had now begun to breathe regularly, at the pieces of ceramic from the broken lamp, and at Kevin's bleeding head.

"Is he dead?"

"Just out," I said begging him with my eyes not to call for help now. He grabbed his pants from the chair, took a cigarette from the night stand, lit it and inhaled deeply while he thought about what to do. Then he reached for the phone.

I helped Kassandra up, grabbed my shoes, and we ran out. On the street, we hailed a cab. Kassandra's lower lip was bleeding, her left eye was already swollen shut and the entire right side of her face and neck was turning purple.

"What was that about?" I asked.

"He wanted to fuck me in the ass. I don't do ass."

"Oh my God, he beat you because of that?"

"Yeah, and because I took his money."

"How much did you take?"

"Everything that was in his wallet."

"He didn't want to pay you?"

"He said he wasn't going to pay up because he didn't get what he wanted. Bastard!"

"You want to go to the hospital?"

"Is it that bad?"

"You might need some stitches on the side of your lip."

"I need a mirror." She leaned over the front seat and asked the driver to let her see the rearview mirror for a moment.

"Naah, I've had worse. We need to find a place to spend the rest of the night. Señor," she said to the driver, "can you please take us to El Malecón motel."

Kassandra took out a wad of money from under her dress. She gave the driver a ten-dollar bill and started counting the rest.

"We have almost a thousand dollars. John had about $300 in his wallet. How was it with him?"

"He came in less than two minutes and passed out."

"I told you how easy it was going to be. If it wasn't for that asshole, we would've made a lot more."

She rolled all the money again and stuck it somewhere. I looked at her questioningly.

"In my crotch," she said, "it's the safest..."

She didn't finish her sentence. She lowered the window and sat back pulling all her hair from her face. The cool night breeze was relaxing. The streets of La Habana were alive with people even though the clock on the dashboard said it was almost six a.m.

When we reached the motel, Kassandra handed me a fifty dollar bill and instructed me to get the room while she waited outside. Her face and neck were full of blood and part of her dress had some as well.

I went in and asked for a room with one bed. The clerk at the front desk said it was fifty dollars, and wanted to ask who the room was for, I could tell. But I didn't give him the chance to. I dropped the fifty-dollars on the counter in front of him. He took the fifty and slid it down his pocket without taking his eyes off me. I took the old fashioned big key from his hand, said thank you and stepped out to meet my friend.

CHAPTER THREE

Kristen was a tiny baby with pretty green eyes like her mother's. Kassandra looked through the glass at the incubator that held her daughter.

"She's so small," she said.

"She'll grow when you start feeding her."

"When are they going to let me take her?"

"I don't know. C'mon, let's find the nurse," I said taking her hand.

The halls of the hospital were dirty, and the paint on the walls was chipping away and collecting in tiny mounds in all the corners. The nurse's station was comprised of a large desk with files on it, a monitor that beeped continuously, and a chair. No one sat in it, and there were people walking around, but few in scrubs.

A short, bald man with glasses wearing a lab coat approached us and asked if he could help. He looked at Kassandra's battered face. We told him we needed to know when the baby in the last incubator was going to be released.

"She's going to need at least one more week," he said. "Are you the mother?" He asked me.

"No, I am," Kassandra said stepping forward.

"She's still drinking very little milk and her blood pressure is not up to par. We need to watch her a little longer." The doctor said with obvious worry in his voice. "What happened to you?"

"I fell. Is she okay? I mean, is there anything wrong with her?"

"She's been tested for everything. The only unclear result is the hearing test. Some premature babies have trouble with the hearing."

"Is she deaf?" Kassandra asked with desperation in her voice.

"We're not sure yet."

"What do you mean you're not sure?"

"She has reacted to some stimuli but not all of them have proven to be..."

"What does that mean?" she interrupted, "don't talk to me like a doctor."

"She hears some things but she doesn't hear others. Where have you been while we've been running these tests?"

She ignored his question. "She's deaf?" I could see the tears peeking in her eyes and heard a knot in her throat.

"She's not completely deaf because she has reacted to some noise. She might just need a hearing aid."

Kassandra started to cry. My heart went out to her. The doctor told us to take a seat in the room next to the incubators. He tried unsuccessfully to cheer her up making sure he told her all the positive things in her daughter being able to hear, at least a little.

"Why did this happen to my little girl, doctor?"

"We don't know. Science can't do anything when it comes to nature's decisions."

"Was it my fault? I had a really bad pregnancy."

"That can sometimes be a factor, but it's not always the case. I've had mothers who have been in bed the entire pregnancy getting up to go only to the bathroom and their babies can hear nothing. With premature babies it's more common because the ears and the lungs are the last things to fully develop."

"I went into labor because I got slapped and fell down."

"Yes, I know. I read the file."

"So she's deaf because of that?"

"You can't take responsibility for that. It wasn't your fault you got slapped. The monster who slapped you is the one responsible."

Kassandra kept crying. I held her tight while the doctor excused himself to attend to his other patients. She stood in front of the glass again, still sobbing. She turned her head every which way to try to see her daughter's face better.

"I'm sorry," she muttered. "I promise I'll make this up to you."

She had her hand against the glass. I knew we should leave at that moment so I took her by the arm and we walked out. It was a beautiful sunny day and we walked aimlessly, in silence, for a long while.

"Do you want to go back to the room?" I asked her as we approached a bus stop.

"We need to figure out what we're going to do for

money tonight."

"Kassandra your face looks like shit."

"My pussy does all the work," she said very serious.

"How are we going to get clients?"

"You're going to get them. You're gonna have to learn on your own. You hook them and get them to agree to the two of us."

"How am I supposed to do that?"

"It's really not that hard. Stand by el malecón and wait until someone approaches you."

"That's all?"

"You have to establish a price right off the bat."

"You don't think we can cover some of that with some make-up?" I pointed to her face.

"You got some? Plus if I even show my face around el malecón, Camacho will be on my ass in no time. I'll be in the room. You just come get me when you get one."

I wasn't even sure how I would "get one." But I didn't want to disappoint her with my questions. I walked across the boulevard, which was filled with pedestrians and bikes, to the wall that prevents the water in the bay from coming into the city.

The famous malecón is usually full of lovers, prostitutes and people looking to make a quick dime. You can find practically anything you want in el malecón. If you want pot, coke, heroin, one or two prostitutes. Whatever your twisted mind desires is available there.

At first, I walked close to the wall, but I kept bumping into people. I decided to walk in the middle of the large sidewalk where the streetlights shone. I must have walked the entire strip when I realized I was at the tail end of it. In front of me was the popular hotel, El Capricho. I remembered Kassandra had mentioned she had found some good clients there.

From the large glass windows, I looked in at the display merchandise; European brands that had to be bought only with dollars. The hotel was busy with people coming in and out of rooms, and I figured no one would notice if I walked in. It is one of the most popular hotel for tourists to take the prostitutes to because it is nice and not too expensive, I could just hear Kassandra saying.

An older man left the front desk and started coming my way. I pretended not to see him, kept on looking at the clothes.

"Excuse me, young lady, are you staying in the hotel?"

"No I'm not," I said.

"Then you must leave."

"I'm just looking at the clothes."

"Go look somewhere else. You can't afford these."

"What if I have dollars to buy them with?"

"I wouldn't sell them to you; you're not a tourist."

"How do you know that?"

He looked up and down at me as if I had leprosy. "It's obvious you're not a tourist. Please save yourself the embarrassment of being manhandled by cops."

I gave him a nasty look, left the lobby and kept on walking aimlessly for another hour. I saw the working girls getting into the newer cars that only tourists could afford. Some were being dropped off, some were negotiating, half bodies in through the windows.

It was six o'clock in the afternoon. My feet hurt and I was losing all hope of finding a client. I decided to go back to the room to rest for a bit and then later, go out again. Kassandra had been standing by the window watching me the entire time.

"I know you don't know how to do this, but use your common sense. If you walk around and see nothing's happening, then you gotta do what some of the girls that are getting picked up are doing."

"Like what? Hang half my body in a car to try to sell it?"

"Yes! Can you do that? Can you sell yourself? That's basically what this business is about."

"My feet hurt."

"My entire face and body hurt. But we have to work!"

"Can't we just take a break tonight? I mean look what happened to us last night for being so desperate!"

I knew I hit a chord, and even though she took some time to think about it, she agreed. "You're right, but only tonight. If we start comiendo mierda, and wasting money instead of making it, we won't have anything."

"I need to make the money too, but I am so tired that I would probably fall asleep in the middle of it."

We laughed. "Most men don't give a shit if you enjoy it or not as long as they get off," she said.

I didn't need to be a jinetera to know that. My

neighbor had never asked or cared if I liked it, I told Kassandra.

"And you weren't a jinetera for him," she said, "that's why every chance you get, you fuck them like they fuck you."

I agreed, crumbling on the bed next to her and thinking about the last two days, how different things were now. Kassandra's voice reverberated in my head. *Now you're a jinetera, you're less than nothing to them, so be smart.*

The next morning Kassandra's eyes were black and blue. The cut on her lip had coagulated blood preventing it from further bleeding. The left portion of her forehead protruded in a horrific egg shaped bump. She complained that her right pinky finger hurt and she could hardly move it.

She sat on the side of the bed inspecting her wounds. I propped my head up in my palm.

"Are you going to be okay to work today?"

"Listen to you," she said standing up. "You sound like me, all you want to do is make money."

"No, I'm worried about you," I said. This stopped her cold; she looked bewildered, as if she couldn't understand these words. The hardcore, beaten up prostitute turned suddenly into a frightened little girl in desperate need of affection.

I sat up intending to go to her but she stepped back

undoing her top. It was then I saw the greenish yellow color of her ribcage, the bruises on her neck, the purplish hand impressions on her forearms.

"Kassandra, I think you need a doctor," I said, now myself on the edge of the bed.

"Yes, to marry me and take me the fuck out of this country," she said, throwing her clothes on the floor and slamming the door of the bathroom behind her.

I threw myself back on the bed and closed my eyes. My mother smiled, not the happy smile of her returning from a trip, but a sad loving and forgiving smile that gnawed at my supposedly non-existent guilt.

What seemed like seconds later, Kassandra stammered out of the bathroom holding her groin area, blood dripping through her fingers. Her thighs were soon covered in blood. The skin on her face was light purple under the injuries; she was about to faint. I ran to her and held her head before it hit the floor. I tried to wake her but her eyes disappeared under her forehead. Panic stricken, I ran out to the hall and screamed for help. Soon, heads were popping out of doors. Minutes later, there were two pairs of shoes in front of me. I had dragged Kassandra's limp body from the door, and rested her head on my thighs.

The men who stood in those shoes were asking questions. How did I know this woman? What was my relationship to her? Had we done any drugs?

"No, we haven't," I screamed looking up at them. "She just got out of the hospital, she needs a doctor."

The two men wore police uniforms. The tall one with a beard and dark beady eyes smiled. The other, older, shorter and fat, pretended to write something on a piece of crumpled up paper as he walked to close the front door.

"Oficiales, por favor ayundenme," I said. Then I remembered the warnings my mother always gave me about policías. Most of them are pigs, she said, like the Americans called them in their movies. I thought the fact that my friend lay almost lifeless in my hands would appeal to whatever humanity was left in them.

"What do we get in return for your help?" the fat one asked.

"Please, whatever you want. Just please help my friend."

"We will help your friend when you tell us what you are doing here?"

"We...we were just, ah, we....she is my girlfriend."

"Tortilleras y putas. We are in luck tonight!" The tall one celebrated.

Before I could say anything, he had scooped me up from under my armpits, and thrown me on the bed. He stepped toward the bed undoing his belt and pants. I had the urge to throw up again, but instinct told me to breathe. If I could not get us out of this, Kassandra would bleed to death. I exhaled, inhaled again. He swiped my right leg to the side. I reached for the condoms in the nightstand. He agreed to put it on only if I did it. After ripping it open, I tried to expand the latex to cover the entire penis, but it only reached halfway. His penis was large and thick.

"Goddamned things! Can't they make them bigger?" He was angry, grabbed his penis, pulled the latex off and stuck it in my mouth. "Cogela tu, mi hermano," he instructed the other cop. The fat one, unsure he should leave Kassandra's side, reluctantly walked over.

"Come on, fuck her!"

I tried to pull back, but the tall one moved for his gun. I raised my hands, took a deep breath because I knew he was going to hit me. Instead, I felt hands on my hips forcing them to bump back against a body. The tall cop, gun in one hand, took the back of my neck and pushed his penis in my mouth again. The other groped around behind me until he ripped the panties off and I felt him enter me. He was not using a condom.

I knew I shouldn't fight them, the more I did, the worse it would be for me. In minutes that seemed like months, the fat one was done. The tall one kept pushing my face against his pelvic bone, pushing his penis all the way down my throat. I could not stop gagging.

"Hurry up, man," the fat cop said, buckling his pants. I felt the penis expand in my mouth, like James's had. With a loud groan, he pulled it out, continued to press my face on it, and ejaculated all over my eyes and cheeks.

The two men started to walk away fixing their clothes. "We'll call for someone to help your friend," the tall one said at the door. They disappeared. I looked at the small puddle of blood forming underneath Kassandra's hips. I cleaned my face and hands with the sheet, ran to take her head in my hands. I shook her, smacked her, begged her to wake up. Her neck wobbled. She was completely out. I placed her head down carefully and ran to the hall screaming for help. No one opened their doors this time. I went back inside with Kassandra. A few minutes went by until I heard the ambulance's roar.

This time the doctor was a middle aged woman with a resilient face; I thought perhaps, due to the many disappointments of the Revolution. Doctors in my country made less money than cab drivers. She explained that Kassandra had bled more than usual.

"It happens sometimes when the mother is too active shortly after the delivery," she said.

"How long until she is released?"

"Let's see how she's doing tomorrow, and maybe we can let her go. Go home now and get some rest, you look tired."

I smiled, looked at my friend again, and whispered a thank you to the doctor as she walked away. Kassandra would have wanted me to work that night. With two days gone, we had twelve days left to get the rest of the money. As the night air hit my face at the double doors of the hospital, I realized how hungry I was. I hailed a cab to the room, showered, dressed, gathered all our stuff, and went down to the lobby. At the front desk, I paid for an additional night but requested a change of room just in case the cops decided to come back. In the new room, I hid all our money under the bathroom sink. I then headed to el malecon to find some food and hopefully a client.

Because most restaurants in the city were "For tourists only" and you had to pay with dollars, some of the locals had begun to cook out of their homes in order to sell the food on the street. Some people sold the items right out of their windows. These were called paladares. I was lucky to find one quickly because I couldn't have walked very long. I felt weak, scared and not really sure how I was going to get a client on my own.

When I finished my pan con bistec, which had no meat at all but a substance with a similar consistency called soya, I paid and left a dollar tip. If there's one thing you learn quickly on the malecon is that if you tip well, they'll remember you. The thick set man behind the window was thankful and said to come back anytime. I had secured a roof and some food; Kassandra would be proud. Finding a client was going to be harder, but I was more confident now that my belly was full.

As I passed the motel, I looked up at the window Kassandra had been looking out of just yesterday afternoon. I remembered the advice on the empty spots along the boulevard. Instead of tiring my feet walking, I picked a spot to watch the jineteras as they got into cars. It was a slow night, none of the women were getting into any vehicles.

On the sidewalk, right against the wall of rocks that prevents the water from rushing in, there were vendors of just about anything. I watched the street hoping one of the women would soon leave an empty spot for me to take. I had stopped at one of the vendors pretending to look at some silver jewelry that was for sale when I heard a familiar voice. From the corner of my eye, I saw the tall policeman from yesterday. My heart sunk, my palms became sweaty, and I was so scared I walked away with the silver ring in my hand.

"Hey, ladrona, come back here with my ring!" a man's voice close behind me said. I turned to give him the ring when the two police officers grabbed my shoulders and took me down to the ground. Instinctively, I fought back. All I could think of was getting away, and that they would have to kill me before they could.

We struggled briefly on the ground, but it all ended when the tall officer put the barrel of his gun on my cheek.

"Stop, puta, or I shoot you right here!"

I knew he would have, and nothing more than a short fake investigation would have followed my untimely death. So I listened and ceased the fighting. He had the back of my head firmly grasping all my hair, and the gun pushing into my face. I put my hands up, my small bag fell, and some of the money I had on me fell out. The fat officer bent to pick it up.

"You must have just come from a punto, look at all the dollars you got," he said counting the few bills.

"I haven't worked yet. Please, that's the only money I got," I said thanking my intuition for not bringing all the money with me.

"Cuanto es?" asked the tall one.

"About fifty pesos and ten dollars," answered the fat one.

"What puta in La Habana takes pesos? You must be a real rookie!"

"I told you I haven't made any money yet. That's all I have."

By now there was a circle of onlookers on the sidewalk. No one said or did anything. They simply watched as the two cops groped around my clothes to see if I had any more money, and took whatever had fallen out. The tall one pushed me back down on the ground holding tightly to my hair as he whispered in my ear.

"I'm checking out what you do. I want half the money you make every night on this street. If not, we're coming back up to your room. And this time we won't be so nice."

I nodded. He pushed my face one more time with the gun, and they were off. I sat there crying, trying to collect the rest of the things that had fallen out of the bag. People dispersed and continued walking. No one stopped to help; no one asked if I was okay; no one even gave me a hand to get up. It was as if what had just taken place was part of the normal day to day operations of the city.

I stood and slowly dragged myself to the short rock wall. My jaw and cheek bones hurt; my knees were scraped, and somehow in the struggle my lip had been cut. I inspected my arms and legs for more wounds.

The will to work and make the money I so desperately needed was gone. I looked at the young women on the boulevard and wondered if they had gone through the same ordeal at the beginning of their careers. It was still slow, no open spots, no one was getting picked up. I sat there for a while realizing that time was passing, and I was losing yet another night.

"Are you okay?" asked a voice in an accented Spanish. A tall, well dressed extranjero stood to my left looking out into the open sea and puffing on a cigarette. I could see the tanned skin of his face, the muscular silhouette of his body and smell the American brand of the cigarette.

"I'm fine now," I said looking down at my knee.

"What happened?" he asked, offering me a Marlboro.

"No, thank you," I said. "You didn't see what happened?"

"I was at the other end and saw the commotion but didn't get here on time to see the whole thing."

He took a small step inhaling deeply on his cigarette without looking my way, he simply stared at the sea. The accent was not German or Swedish, but not American either.

"Are you American?" I asked.

"American parents but I was born and live in Canada."

"I charge in dollars," I said hastily, almost desperately.

He turned to face me, took the cigarette from his lips, exhaled, and without saying anything looked back at the water.

"I have dollars," he said after a few seconds.

"One hundred dollars."

He nodded now looking directly at me. "How old are you?"

"Nineteen. That's for two hours, okay, mister?"

He took another drag of his cigarette while smiling at me. I smiled back, looked at my dangling feet.

"I wasn't looking for that tonight," he said.

"What you are looking for then?"

"I was just going for a walk."

"You don't like me?"

"I'm thinking about it."

This is where Kassandra would have jumped on him, nibbled something on his ear, taken his hand and dragged him to a room. I didn't know what to do now. I needed the money but didn't want him to know how dreadfully.

"No much think about. These women not as pretty as me."

"Maybe you're just too young."

"Young is good, no, Mr.?"

"Too young is not. You can call me Martin."

"I told you I'm nineteen. That's no too young."

"How about if we make a deal?" he asked. Here it was; he was going to counteroffer. I couldn't say no to whatever he offered because something was better than nothing. "How about if you spend the next three days with me, and I pay you a thousand dollars?"

I thought I had heard wrong. "Qué?"

"One thousand dollars for three days with me,

starting tonight."

I had been taught since I was a child that if something was too good to be true, it probably wasn't all that good. This man was probably some sort of psycho or sick individual that got off in twisted ways. Then I thought about the boat that would be leaving in another week or so. A thousand dollars for three days was probably more than I would make walking the malecon on my own. I needed to show Kassandra that I could do this for us, that I, like her, was just as desperate to get out of the island.

And if she was released from the hospital, maybe the money would double.

"I have friend, she's really pretty. Maybe you want two for three days, same price for her?"

"I'm fine with just you." He was still looking at the water inhaling his cigarette. I looked around. The jineteras looked irritated at the lack of potential clients. These women would tear me apart if I took a spot that was theirs or belonging to one of their friends because I was an unfamiliar face. I'd never even been in a fight at school. I wished my friend was with me.

"Okay, but I don't do freaky stuff, okay? No anal sex."

"I'm not into that."

"Why you pay so much?"

"You think a thousand dollars for three days is a lot?"

"I ah...I think I ah..."

"Don't worry, I'm not a pervert nor do I like weird

things. I'm here on business for about a week. If you spend the next three days with me and show me the island, I'll have a better sense where I'm investing my money."

I knew an American or a Canadian businessman was the luckiest thing that could happen to me at this point, and Kassandra would scream at me if I didn't take this opportunity.

"Where do you stay?" I asked.

"El Nacional."

El Nacional was the best hotel on the strip. At a minimum of $300 a night, not many of the jineteras ever visited it. I took a moment to look at the ocean wondering if my mother's spirit along with La Virgen de Regla was looking at me from the waves. Nothing. Kassandra was right. I no longer felt anything other than the excitement of the money.

"Let's go then." I said jumping off the wall and threading my arm through his. He gave me a broad smile and this time I saw two rows of perfect white teeth. The dim reflection of the street lights showed eyes with light corneas but I could not tell whether they were blue or green. "You have car?"

"Back at the hotel. I like to walk."

As we walked in the direction of the hotel, I could feel the angry looks from the women on the street. They'd probably been standing there for hours without any luck. I didn't even glance their way. I kept my eyes on the floor, occasionally looking up at him not believing how lucky I was. Half a block down, he asked my name.

"What do you want it to be?" I said remembering Kassandra's charm and trying to imitate it.

"I want it to be your real name. What your mother calls you."

"She doesn't call me anything anymore. She's dead," I said.

"I'm sorry. What did she call you?

"Milena."

"How did she die?"

"On a raft," I said.

He waited for more, but when I didn't say anything else, he patted my fingers that were holding onto his arm. "It's okay, we have a lot of time to get to know each other."

Why he wanted to get to know me was beyond me. Most of the customers never really care to know anything about you, I remembered Kassandra saying. Unless they were lonely or something.

"Are you lonely, Martin?" I regretted asking this question as soon as I had completed the sentence. He stopped walking, took a few more steps toward the wall, and rested against it taking out another cigarette.

"I'm sorry," I said, quickly realizing I had touched a delicate subject and ran the risk of losing the client.

"It's fine," he said, lighting the cigarette. "I am lonely."

"You miss your family in Canada?"

"Don't have one. I guess we have a lot in common," he said. "You don't have to say anything," he continued, resuming his pace on the boulevard."

This time I walked without threading my arm through his and looked at the floor all the time. Kassandra would say Yemaya was looking down at me somehow trying to show I was still her daughter by sending me this opportunity. I walked without saying a word, wondering if I was in fact lucky. Martin walked quietly, occasionally glancing my way. I was thankful for his silence.

CHAPTER FOUR

S ex with Martin was slow, soft, delicate. I had not expected him to be rough, but his hands trembled, as if afraid to touch my skin. He took a very long time to be ready and several times he had to stop, go to the bathroom, and come back. I asked him what was wrong but he said nothing, he hadn't been with a woman so young in a long time and he felt somewhat pressured.

I was skeptical, wondered if there was something else, something weird he'd want me to do. But after we had eaten breakfast, he said I should go down to the stores in the lobby to buy a dress for tonight.

I didn't ask any questions. On the nightstand, there were three one hundred dollars bills beside a plastic room key. Under the sheets, I stretched my body on the huge bed then looked out the window.

"I enjoyed you last night," he said, fixing his tie.

"I did too," I responded, not sounding too convincing.

"Make sure you get a nice dress. I'll be back by two."

I nodded again, and as he left the room I wondered if today they would release Kassandra and Kristen from the hospital. I got up, put my clothes on, grabbed the money and the room key. I didn't stop in the lobby but outside hailed a cab to my own motel. I shuddered at the thought of bumping into the cops there, but with little options as to places to stay in el malecon, I had no other choice.

After showering and dressing in some more of Kassandra's clothes, I went down to pay for another night. The clerk behind the front desk examined the hundred dollar bill.

He looked at me and said, "Good night last night, huh?"

I was repulsed by the grin on his face and his beady eyes that reminded me of the tall cop, but I only said "great" knowing it was worthless for me to answer anything else.

I took my change and walked outside. On the sidewalk, I waited for the bus to the hospital. I had little choice now that I was officially what Castro called the scum of the earth in his speeches. My tia and the few friends I had left would not want to be associated with a jinetera. My heart ached for my mother who was surely looking down at me, unhappy with my decision. But when I was able to get out, to live in a country where I could be somebody, she'd be proud of me. This was my only consolation.

Kassandra would not be released today. She had severe anemia, bronchitis and splitting headaches. The woman doctor with the stern face said maybe in two days, if her lungs cleared. The baby was doing much better though; she slept peacefully in her manmade womb.

I told Kassandra about Martin.

"When you go back, go through the room, see

what you find about him."

"I don't feel comfortable doing that."

"He gave you a key! So he trusts you or he's testing you. Maybe both. You could go through his things, just don't take anything."

"I wouldn't take anything anyway."

"Listen to me, be very smart with this client. He could be another way out of here."

"What do you mean? We're out of here in a week or so. When you get well, you go back to work, we'll—"

"Shhhh…" he signaled for me to lower my voice. "What if we can't come up with the money? I had a good friend who met an older extranjero. She fucked his brains out. He married her and took her to Rome. She divorced him two years later and now lives with her Cuban boyfriend in Naples, the one in la Yuma, not Italy."

"He's probably fifty something, too old for me," I said, incredulous at her ability to talk about marriage so lightly. My mother used to tell me that she didn't care who I married, as long I loved him. Marriage was serious. We were prostitutes.

"The older they are the better; the more they fall in love with you," she said.

I had not thought about the possibility of Martin really falling in love with me. He had taken his time with me, been courteous and almost sweet. But there was a silent coldness about him that was unsettling.

"I've only known him one night! Maybe tonight he's a jerk."

"From what you've told me, he's a good one. I wish I would've found him."

"I think I can convince him to pay the two of us for the week."

"Don't push it now; I can't get out of here anyway. Just make sure he enjoys himself in everything he does with you, and be yourself. Remember you are a descendant of Yemaya; she's with you."

I had been evoking La Caridad del Cobre because she was my mother's saint, and Ochun is one of the most powerful saints. He is a guerrero, a warrior that fights for his people. But Yemaya was the one that supposedly looked out for me, so on the crowded bus that rode over the pot holes on the streets of La Habana, I said a prayer to La Virgen de Regla believing the one that would answer was her African counterpart.

I had to believe a blessing from her was finding Martin since Kassandra would be in the hospital for at least another three days, and I wouldn't have to face the streets on my own. I'd spend the three days with him, then when she was out, I'd go back to regular work with her guidance. I knew I couldn't handle walking el malecon by myself again.

The lobby of El Nacional was clean, with expensive modern furniture decorating it and filled with tourists everywhere. There were two stores of clothes and shoes, a hair salon, a bathing suit store, a jewelry store, and at the far end, near the elevators, a thick door led to the spa, and the pool. I'd never been in a hotel where you had anything you needed right in the lobby, no need to step out. I marveled at how the tourists were treated like royalty and quickly found out the difference between them and us.

"Excuse me," a man's voice came from behind. I window shopped a gold and black cocktail dress rimmed with fine tulle. "You're going to have to leave." The bald and short man had a feminine manner about him. His hands moved gracefully and explanatory.

"I need to buy that dress," I said pointing at the mannequin.

"You know you can't. Now please leave."

"But I have money," I said bringing the proof to light. "And a friend of mine is staying here."

"A friend?" he asked with a suspicious grin. "What is your friend's name?"

"Martin."

"Martin what?"

I had not gotten Martin's last name. He had mentioned something about it not being French but had not said it.

"I don't know his last name."

"You don't know your friend's last name?"

"I just told you I don't."

"What's the room number?"

"I don't know the number, but here's the key."

"You don't know the room number, you don't know his last name, you could've gotten that key from anywhere."

"I was in a hurry when I left." I had not looked at the door when I left, but thought that with only four other rooms in this portion of the hall, I'd be able to find my way back.

"Ms. Whatever your name is," he said looking closely at the key, "I'm not going to waste my time. Please leave or I will be forced to call the police."

"Why won't you just test the key? I'm telling you the truth!" I said in a raised voice.

He looked around to see if anyone had heard me and said under his breath, "I'm not going to have a jinetera scream at me in my lobby. Now leave before I call the police!"

I knew the battle was lost before it had begun. I gave him a look that spelled hate, turned on my heel and left. Outside, I cried. I had to lean against the wall, wipe my face with the sleeve of Kassandra's flowered blouse, and take a minute to look at the long street ahead.

I had three hours before Martin got back. I started to walk thinking if I should just go to my room and stay in there until about 1:30 when I would take a cab back to the hotel and wait until I saw Martin walk in.

Without realizing how long I had walked, I ended up at the edge of the walkway between the water and the boulevard. Even at this hour, the boulevard was filled with unlicensed vendors, jineteras, and tourists who looked eagerly at the beautiful waters of the bay. Like them, I stared at the waves swaying in from the Atlantic, softly crashing against the coral wall on a perfect blue sky background.

The sun had started to heat the pavement, and the reflection of it made the boulevard a mirage onto which forty-year-old cars rode, buses stuffed with smelly Cubans, and where Canadians, Spanish and Swedish businesses thrived. When I was a little girl, my mother told me stories of the Spaniards and how a hundred years ago a rich Spaniard had had a love affair with a beautiful African and that was where her family had gotten the black in us. I wished she knew more about my family, about the slave times, about the Spaniards who had been my ancestors and the Africans who'd given me my skin color.

Sluggishly, I walked half a block. A family of Cubans was sharing a guarapo, a sweet shake from the sugar cane, at a paladar. I looked at them with a twinge of envy. Although you could tell they had nothing, they had each other. A mother, a father, and the two teenage boys. They wore cheap Russian-made clothes, the boys had old sneakers and the father wore torn high tops from the decade before. The mother, who had had a pretty face in her youth, wore sandals with the sequins scaling off and an old topless beach dress.

The entire family was thin, almost gaunt, and their faces were dry, with the haunting look of the hungry and desperate. But they stood there, sharing their one glass of guarapo and everything seemed to be fine with them.

From behind me, a man's voice yelled an incomprehensible slur. The voice was coming from a dark corner of a memory, but devoid of a face. I turned, slowly, fear penetrating my bones. It was Camacho holding a young girl by her mane of dark brown curls. He was visibly drunk, his plaid shirt open, hanging loosely on his thin body. She struggled to free herself from the grip, to no avail. He pushed her face down into the pavement, and continued to yell, himself now on his knees, the yelling closer to her face. When I saw him do this to Kassandra, I knew it had not been the first time, this was how he operated with all his jineteras. Foolishly, without further thought, I jumped in the middle of them.

"Leave her alone, you piece of shit," I said, with a fearless voice I didn't even know I had.

Camacho looked up at me. Even in his stupor, he couldn't believe someone had talked to him in that tone of voice.

"Who the fuck are you?" he said trying to retain the girl's hair while raising half his body to confront me.

"Leave her alone," I repeated.

"Or what?" he said stumbling forward on his attempt to stand.

"Or I'll call the cops!"

"Call the cops, you stupid cunt. You'll be in jail in less than twenty minutes." And once on his feet, he launched his hands at my face. I took a quick step sideways, and he rocketed into the bay wall. The girl was quick on her feet and took off running. I was tempted to follow her but decided to go the opposite way, within a split second my body was running. Camacho tried helplessly to run after me but fell on his face, ass up, hands by his side. I looked back, saw that he was on the ground, slowed down to a jog towards Martin's hotel. As I got closer, I knew it was no use to try to go in again. I walked slowly by the front of the lobby, stopping briefly to look at the dress I wanted. I knew the moment I'd walk in, the bald headed man would have me kicked out. I kept on walking, deciding on the entrance by the back. Most of the big hotels had pools in the back, and sometimes, people left the gates open. If you got caught, my mother used to say, tell them you're with the dance group; no one really knew who they were, but personnel always left you alone after that.

It was early enough, and if I could get into the hotel and in the elevator, I would undoubtedly remember which door was Martin's room. The back entrance was protected by a metal fence a little more than six feet tall. The flimsy gate had a thick padlock on it that protected a spectacular Olympic size pool adorned with two rock waterfalls. Under the rocks, guests could rent the small cabanas for a minimum of one hour. The waterfalls gave the cabanas complete privacy, access to a full bar and a waitress. On the other side were chairs and umbrellas. There were a few people lying out on them, but scattered about the length of the pool. I watched some of them jump in, come out, some went into a door at the far end. I assumed it was the bathroom or the lobby. If I could get in there, I could easily slip into the elevator.

Without hesitation, I threw my shoes over, laced my fingers through the cold metal and jammed my toes into the small squares. I climbed to the top, looked down to the side, carefully threw one leg over, then the other. It was easier than I thought it would be. A palm tree covered me and no one had seen me climb over, otherwise hotel security would be here by now.

I quickly put my shoes on and pretended to be strolling about the pool. It was well known that if you were caught in the pool or the lobby of any hotel, especially in La Habana, you were at best kicked out, or put in jail. I walked in, looked for the elevator and started to walk towards it. A huge pair of arms tackled me from the left side. Both of our bodies fell, his on top of mine. The oxygen from my lungs escaped as I gasped for air and passed out.

When I came to, my head ached and my body throbbed in pain. I was on a plastic chair in a small gray room with a metal door. My legs were somewhat numb, my fingers were prickly. I was still wearing the same clothes, but no shoes. My feet hurt. I touched my face, my jaw hurt, and realizing that this time something bad had happened, I started to cry. Just then the metal door sprung open, a tall, balding man with wiry glasses wearing a suit waltzed in. He didn't say hello, didn't even look my way. He dropped a bunch of files at my feet, stared at them. I waited for him to say something, when he didn't, I asked where I was and who was he.

"You're in the security office of the hotel. I'm the head of security."

"I have a friend who's staying here."

"Yes, that seems to be your story."

"I have a key in my purse, and his name is Martin.

Please just look him up and you'll see I'm not lying."

"Why were you trying to come in the back way?"

"Because the manager didn't believe me."

"There's no key in your purse, we've looked. And as far as a guest named Martin, we need the last name to find him in the registry."

"What do you mean there's no key? He gave me the key this morning before he left to a business meeting. I'm supposed to meet him back here at two o'clock."

"This friend Martin, do you see him often?"

I knew I needed to be careful how I answered his questions. I was dressed like a jinetera, and my story was a jinetera's dream.

"Uh huh." I mumbled.

"How often?"

"Whenever he's in La Habana?"

"Where is he from?"

I hesitated because I remembered Martin said he had American parents but he lived in Canada. But did that make him American? In any case, a Canadian was a better choice than an American.

"Canada," I said.

"You know he's Canadian but you don't know his last name? How do you two know each other?" The sarcasm in his voice was annoying.

"Business partners," I said with the same level of irony.

"What kind of business?"

"Can I have a glass of water?"

"When you tell me what kind of business you two

are involved in."

"He's looking into opening up a restaurant for me to run." I pulled that lie out of nowhere, but I remembered Kassandra mentioned that restaurants did better than any other businesses because the one thing that people had to do every day was eat.

"Can I have a glass of water now, please?"

He took a step back, stared at the files in front of my feet for a second more and stepped out. I looked down at the files. I wanted to leaf through them to see what they were, but wasn't sure if that was a good move. With the tip of my big toe, I moved the one on top. It fell over the pile. I bent to open it. There were hundreds of mug shots of women. I closed it quickly and put the file on top again; I heard steps outside the door.

He walked in, looked at the files, handed me the paper cup with water, and reclined against the wall. I gulped the water. My head was pounding and my stomach grumbled.

"Did you find yourself in there?" he asked.

"What do you mean?"

"I see you went through them. Did you find your picture in there?"

"I didn't go through them. And why would my picture be in there?"

"Because those are police files of all the jineteras in the city. We looked for yours but didn't find it. Your name isn't on the list either. So you must have been using another name when you got caught."

"I've never been in trouble with the law."

"How long have you been jineteando?"

They didn't have my picture or my name, so they knew nothing for sure and like the cops in the American movies, they just assumed I'd tell them.

"What makes you think I'm a jinetera?"

"The way you're dressed, the way you were trying to sneak in here."

"I told you why I was trying to get in here, and I'm dressed to go out."

"At noon?"

I gulped the last of the water. Stared at him, looked down at the files again. He waited, like the patient alligator waits for the bird to dive into the water. I leaned on the back of the chair, waited as well.

"All right then, since you've never been arrested, this experience will serve as your first. I'm going to have to call for them to take you to jail."

"But I wasn't doing anything."

"How about trespassing?"

I thought about the "I'm part of the dance company" excuse, but it was too late now. And he would know for sure if there was a dance company or not at the hotel.

"I was just trying to get back to my friend's room. I'm supposed to meet him there at two. Please, just let me wait for him in here and you'll see I'm not lying to you."

"I can't do that. This is one of the finest hotels in the city; we have a lot of people coming in and out, and I can't spend the next two hours in here with you.

I have a job to do, so the sooner you become someone else's problem, the better."

"You can just leave me in here until two. I won't try anything, I promise."

Just then a slight reflection of goodness appeared in his face. "How old are you anyway?" he asked.

I looked at my feet, the files were slightly off one side. If I lied, he would eventually find out and he'd think I was lying about everything.

"Sixteen."

"Where are your parents?"

"Dead."

"Brothers? Sisters?"

I said no with my head. He scratched his jaw, looked pitifully at me. "No one at all?"

I was tempted to tell him about Tia Susi. He would probably get her down to the station, and then she'd be forced to take me home. I didn't want her to have to be responsible for me again. We waited, though I wasn't sure for what. Then he stepped out again, and within seconds was back with another plastic chair, which he straddled.

"Listen, all you have for ID is your word. All you have to prove the Canadian story is your word. So why don't you just come clean with me. I can tell good people from bad ones. Just be honest and I'll help you out."

It was a trap, and I knew it right away. If I confessed to being a jinetera he would have me cuffed and ready to go down to the station in no time. I remembered my mother telling me never to trust the police, Kassandra saying I needed to be smarter now that I depended on no one but myself, and Martin saying if I had any problems, I could just say his name.

"I have been telling you the truth."

"Very well then," he said standing up, "we'll take you down and register you. Since you're a minor, do you have any one that could come get you out?"

I looked at him in disbelief. He was really going to have me arrested. Unless...

"I told you I didn't. Couldn't you and I work something out?"

"I don't work things out with girls like you," he said despondently.

I did my best imitation of Kassandra's flirting technique where she's serious and looks intently into the eyes of her prey. His were a graying greenish color, and I could see the lines around them. Maybe forty-four, maybe forty-five, I thought.

I stood, walked over to him slowly. He stood as well, put the chair between us as a barrier. I walked around it seductively, put my hands inside his suit and caressed his chest. He was frozen in place.

"Stop that," he said grabbing my wrists and pushing my hands away from his chest. "I'm married, and that's not going to work with me."

Married men are easier, they usually don't get a lot of sex at home, I could hear Kassandra's voice in my head.

"How long have you been married?"

"Longer than you've been alive," he said stepping back to put some distance between us.

"Aren't you bored? I can be lots of fun." I wasn't even sure how I would be lots of fun, but what I needed right now was for him to give in; the rest wouldn't be that difficult to figure out.

For a moment, I thought I had him. He looked at me, at my thin body, at my bare feet, and I thought he was going to go for it right in the suffocating room. But then he looked up at the roof, took a deep breath, looked at my eyes. I knew immediately he wasn't interested in sex.

"Why so sad?" I asked.

"Because my job is so much harder when it's a young girl like you."

"Then just let me go, please. I can't go to jail."

"I can't lose my job."

"You can just say you didn't see my picture in there," I pointed at the files with my jaw, "and you had to let me go."

"That's not procedure."

"Señor," I said looking at the floor, "we all break procedural rules." I thought I saw a glint of self-pity in him. I changed strategies.

"My mother drowned trying to leave. She used to spend entire days planning and plotting different ways. I need a better way." Almost everyone in La Habana, especially people in civil service, at one point or another had thought about leaving.

"If I knew a way," he started to say when the metal door opened. The bald headed manager walked in, looked at both of us knowing he had walked in the middle of something.

"Perdón," he said, "there are two policemen outside wanting to speak with you?"

"You called them?"

"No. They're looking for someone," he said looking right at me.

The security guy briskly walked out. The manager gave me a look that spelled disgust. I didn't care. I knew the cops were looking for me, and if pressed, the man whom I had almost witnessed a breakdown from would have no qualms turning me in. The manager walked out slamming the door behind him. I looked around the windowless room. If it was true what Kassandra had told me about Camacho's influence with the police, I was as good as dead. The two pigs outside could take me wherever they pleased, do with me as they wished and dispose of me like a trash bag. No one but Kassandra would ever miss me, and no one would ever know what happened to me. I had to think of something fast.

Had the door been locked from the outside? Knowing the chances were slim, I tried the handle. It gave in easily and the metal door squeaked open. My heart beat faster than I'd ever felt it, but I didn't hesitate. I poked my head out the edge of the door and saw only a few tourists around. I walked out and turned toward the exit to the pool.

There were more people in the pool, more waitresses, more staff altogether walking around. I was scared, shoeless, tears on my cheeks, and sure that someone would soon grab me. But the tourists just looked at me as if part of the scenery, and the staff ignored me. I did not dare to glance back, just walked, fast but not running, reached the gate and pulled. Locked.

CHAPTER FIVE

Barefooted and hungry, I now walked on the opposite side of the boulevard trying to be as inconspicuous as possible. A difficult task when you walk barefooted on the streets of a major city. I had had to climb the same fence to get out of the hotel. Ironic, I thought. Now on the widely popular avenue, I hid my face as best I could. I looked away from people who looked at me, and walked as fast as possible. I could feel the stares and hear the whispers, but I didn't care, I knew I looked a mess. I wanted to get to my room; that was all. The faster I walked, it seemed the farther the motel was. I had done this walk enough times to know that the motel was exactly thirty minutes on foot from the hotel. The restaurant and the paladares were busy with people trying to get food. My stomach grumbled, but I kept walking.

At the traffic light before the motel, a car took the red light and turned right almost running me over. I fell back into the ditch, landing on my hip. The pain was excruciating and I could barely move. Some German tourists (I could distinguish the accent) helped me and sat me down on the sidewalk as a small crowd gathered around me asking what happened. Someone gave me some water. I asked for help getting up but they insisted I stay seated. One of the Germans took out a cell phone and by his motions he was telling me he was calling the ambulance.

I said, "No don't do that! I'm fine, I'm okay." I tried getting up by myself to show them I was fine when a sharp pain ran through my leg and I fell back down. The German dialed. Within minutes, faster than I'd ever heard an ambulance show up on the streets of La Habana, they had me on a stretcher, which was quickly swallowed by the back of the truck. Now I was pleading to be let go, not to be taken to the hospital again. But the medic, a young kid of about twenty with big dark blue eyes, kept pushing me back down and saying, "tranquila, tranquila."

The same hospital with the same crowded lobby, same underpaid and frustrated health professionals; this time it was a different me from the week before. As soon as they put the stretcher against the side of the wall and left me there until a nurse would get to me, I slithered off and dragged my left hip to the elevator. I couldn't make it back to the motel with my leg the way it was. I could, however, stay with Kassandra in her room until the pain subsided a bit and I could call Martin's hotel from the nurse's station.

The hallway on Kassandra's floor was still deserted. Her door was closed but I walked in without knocking. Beside the bed, tightly squeezing Kassandra's neck was Camacho. Kassandra, whose face was red and about to pass out, tried to yell for me to run. I felt no pain from my leg, no fear, only anger. This time, I jumped on top of him and started hitting him furiously. I bit the side of his face and as the pain hit him, he threw me off his back. I landed against the wall, on my hip again. Camacho held his cheek while running in circles like a madman. Kassandra tried to regain her breath. The nurse walked in the middle of all this.

"What is going on here?" she yelled.

Camacho immediately straightened up and pointed a bloody finger at me. "She's crazy, enfermera, she bit my face!"

I had not realized a small chunk of flesh had come off his face. My teeth must have still been biting down when he threw me off.

"You?" the nurse said. "What is the matter with you? Have you gone insane?"

"He was trying to kill my friend!" I yelled.

"Kill her friend? She's nuts. This is my girlfriend; we just had a baby."

Kassandra, still visibly shaken up and trying to get her breath, looked at him in disbelief. "She's not your baby," she managed to say between breaths.

The nurse was confused. She poked her head out of the room quickly and screamed for help in the hall. Within seconds, she was back in front of us. Camacho still held his face, Kassandra tried to get out of the bed and I forced my body up. My leg, now completely numb, dragged on behind me like a dead animal. I came close to the nurse, begging her to help. She held on to my waist, helped me walk outside and sat me onto a chair. She then paged a doctor over the aging PA system. She went back to the room leaving me in pain, being watched by another nurse.

Tiny stabs attacked my lower leg while the throbbing pain in my hip persisted. The nurse now watching me had little emotion on her face. She went about her business in the station without flinching. She didn't ask what happened; she didn't ask where it hurt. It was as if I wasn't there. I asked her for a pill to kill the pain. She said as soon as I saw the doctor, she would give me whatever he wanted me to take.

The doctor, this time a young black man, finally showed up and asked what had happened. I told him. He said he'd need to take an x-ray to make sure I hadn't fractured my hip. My hip wasn't fractured, I assured him, because I wouldn't be able to walk if it was. He saw the logic in this but said I needed to remain still. And with that, he walked toward the room.

My nurse vigilante was not too interested in me. She left the station a couple of times returning a minute or two later. The next time she'd take off, I'd take the elevator down. The pain was subsiding a bit but I couldn't walk fast, and it would take me more than a couple of minutes to reach the damn thing even if it was only a few feet away. There were no exit doors anywhere, only a window at the end of one of the two halls that stretched out from the station. The window at the end of the other hall was blocked with an ancient machine used to hold broken limbs up.

The gray counters of the station were topped with papers everywhere. Just then, the bell of the elevator door went off. Out came two officers who thankfully weren't the same pigs. I sat very still, holding my breath almost, praying to La Virgen de Regla for them not to notice me. They walked past me without a glance. As soon as I saw their backs, I staggered toward the elevator. The door was a foot from closing, and I managed to stick an arm in to push it back. I squiggled into it, pressed the first door button, and waited for the door to close.

The quick ride four floors down gave me time to breathe, but not enough to figure out what my next move would be. As soon as that door opened again and I set foot out on the lobby, the two pigs who had violated me grabbed both of my arms and pushed me down on the floor. The all too familiar position made me want to throw up.

"Look at this, compañero," the tall one said. "We didn't have to go up to look for her; she came right down to us." He celebrated while pushing my face down on the cold, unclean floor. He grabbed the back of my neck, stood me up in one swift move, and cuffed my hands behind my back.

"Don't fight me, puta, this time I won't be so nice."

I went with it, refusing or fighting would only make things worse for me. Within minutes, I was in the back of an old patrol car. The fat cop plopped behind the wheel, the tall one on the passenger seat. He looked back at me.

"You got some guts, puta. You didn't think we would eventually find you?"

I ignored him, looked out the window trying to hold back tears that would undoubtedly please him. My leg was completely numb from the waist down. My wrists and face hurt, and the bottom of my feet were covered with a slimy substance.

The tall cop pushed his body between the two front seats, reached behind, and slapped me so hard that the left side of my face hit the window.

"Don't ignore me when I talk to you, puta. You should learn to respect me."

Now I cried from the pain, the humiliation, the complete helplessness. My mother's face was in my head. Pieces of her memory drifted in and out. I closed my eyes to remember her face better. My brain could only detect the pain from the slap, and now, the stabbing pain from my leg again. Within minutes, I was being dragged out onto the sidewalk and into La Habana police station where I would spend an entire week in a tiny cell with three other jineteras who took my bread in the mornings, part of my lunch in the afternoons, and sometimes my entire dinner. They were much older and seemed to be good friends from the outside, so I didn't argue, didn't fight, but spent my days sitting in a corner with my eyes closed praying to all the Santeria gods and all the catholic saints. My hip healed somewhat, but every now and then shards of pain shot up my spine.

Praying didn't work quickly enough. But after a week, I was released in the afternoon with not so much as a word said to me. I knew the room at the motel was gone, and going back to the hospital was not an option. Kassandra could've been released and other than going to La Habana Vieja to her padrino's house, I had no idea where to find her.

I sat on the edge of el malecon contemplating jumping in to join my mother in the vast ocean. I regretted leaving my tia Susi's house where I at least had had a roof over my head. I regretted the choice I had made when I decided to follow Kassandra in her line of work. In a few weeks I'd be seventeen, two years less than the general population deemed the right age to become a prostitute. In La Habana, nineteen determined a woman's time to make decisions of prostituting herself or going to work for pennies a month, if she was able to find work. Less than nineteen was considered way too young, but everyone was aware that most nineteen year old jineteras had started a few years before.

I thought about Martin, how he must have thought I was a flake for not showing up. Thought about Kristen and Kassandra, and that they had probably been released. Without Kassandra, there wasn't much of a chance that I was ever going to make it to Miami. I didn't know anyone who had any connections to a way out, and even if I did, there was little chance now of me making any money on this street.

Fully aware that there wouldn't be another Martin waiting for me at the malecon, I walked aimlessly about. Somehow, I needed to make it back to the motel even if it was risky. But I needed clothes, money, food. Hopefully, the cops weren't around at this time.

At the motel, the dark-haired woman with wrinkles in her cheeks and upper lip who stood behind the front desk did not recognize me. She didn't know who Kassandra was or when the general manager would come in again. As I briefly explained my situation, she looked at me with a thread of pity in her dark brown eyes.

After a long thoughtful pause, she said, "You can take a shower upstairs; my sister's paladar is around the corner. I'll send for some food."

I thanked her trying not to let the tears roll. This was proof that there was still some good in my people, even if all I had been shown in the last few weeks was the greed and nastiness of an urban society with a thriving tourism industry from which its own citizens cannot legally profit.

I followed her behind the counter to a barbacoa- a makeshift second floor common in the city's small businesses and most homes-which was connected by a wooden ladder.

"The bathroom's on the second floor," she explained handing me a towel. "Go back down and take the other stairs up. I'll bring you some clothes."

I was never more thankful to Yemaya for sending me this complete stranger who was willing to help me. Before she left, I grabbed her hand and kissed it. She smiled, rescued her hand quickly, and disappeared down the wooden ladder. The barbacoa had a bed, a small refrigerator and an old television set sitting on a domino table. The space was no more than three feet in height and about ten in width; if you stood up straight, your head hit the ceiling. I went down the unsteady ladder carefully.

After I showered, she gave me a bag of clothes and a pair of old sneakers. I asked her name.

"Margot," she said, "but you didn't get all this from me, okay?"

I nodded, smiled as I put on the clothes acknowledging the all too familiar fear of the government Cuban people are so accustomed to feeling. There was someone outside the door. Margot went out, quickly came back in with bread soaked in oil and sprinkled with tiny pieces of garlic, an orange soda and a napkin.

"Sorry this isn't much, but it'll keep you moving."

I said thank you stuffing the bread in my mouth. Cuban bread with garlic, oil and salt had been one of my mother's favorite sandwiches while she'd watch me eat the last piece of chicken or steak.

"You gotta go when you're done eating. But come back when you find some work, and I'll give you a break on a room."

"I need one more thing, please. Last week I stayed in one of the rooms here, and I left something in it. I need to just go in and get it; it'll take me less than five minutes."

I had not mentioned what I did for a living, had no need to. Margot dealt with jineteras and their clients day in and out; she had taken one look at me and known. The truth was, I didn't really care who knew and who didn't anymore; where before I felt ashamed of the choices I had made, now the only thing I cared about was saving Kristen and leaving with Kassandra to Miami. The instinct to survive was much more powerful than the guilt and regret. Margot's kindness had awakened a sense of trust I thought lost in me.

"Whatever you left there is gone by now."

"It was hidden. It might still be there."

She thought about this for a moment. "You got exactly five minutes. What was the room number?"

I told her, and minutes later she came back with a key. "It's empty," she said, "but you still need to get out quickly."

I nodded and went up the stairs. Under the sink, between the wood and the water pipe where I had stashed the money, there was now a small wooden piece covering the hole. My heart sunk. I locked the room and went down.

"Thank you," I said to Margot.

"Did you find it?" she asked.

I said no with my head and wiped a tear. She came close, hugged me and said things would eventually get better. They always did.

"Why are you so nice to me?" I asked her.

"I had a daughter. She left the house one day without any goodbyes. They found her body along with twenty others off the coast of Oriente."

"They never found my mother," I said, as if that was any consolation for her daughter. "Sometimes I still have hope."

"Hope is good; it keeps the spirit sane."

Just then I realized how much she looked like my mother. Her café con leche complexion with the big brown eyes that told all, the lines in her face that affirmed an unhappy life. Her words were like my mother's, positive and reassuring.

"Go on now," she said putting some pesos in my hand. "You can't be here long. Just make sure you remember me when you get to Miami."

A contagiously hopeful smile radiated across her face. I gave her the strongest hug I could muster, and kissed her cheek. A couple of tears escaped her eyes; she wiped them quickly and unceremoniously.

Once back on the street, I began thinking of what my next step should be. I could go back to La Habana Vieja to find Kassandra and risk finding Camacho as well. I could try to find my own clients, but all the good spots in the malecon were taken. I had to somehow get to the other side of the city where the competition wasn't so cutthroat but the clients weren't so plentiful. I counted the money Margot had given me. Twenty pesos. It would feed me one more day, maybe two if all I ate was bread and garlic sandwiches. Or I could use it to buy some used shoes to replace the old sneakers Margot had given me. The clothes fit okay, they weren't trendy but they were good quality, definitely American or European. The sneakers however were dirty and ragged, and everyone knows jineteras work in heels.

I jumped on a crowded bus that took me to La Habana Vieja. I bought a pair of cheap black pumps that cost ten pesos from a woman on a corner doing a garage sale because she had won the visa lotto and would be leaving in just a few days. I envied her. I had eight pesos left, enough money for transportation for the next day or two. I sat on a bench in a park where the passersby were in too much of a hurry to look at me. In this part of the city, it was more common to see young people drinking and hanging out than tourists and jineteras. But I didn't have much of a choice. If I worked the malecon, I'd surely bump into Camacho and the two pigs. No one knew my face on this side of the city.

After scanning my whereabouts for some time, I decided a client was not just going to approach me. I had to approach him. There were plenty of lone men who walked by, but not one looked my way. On the malecon, everyone looked at me, including other working girls. Here, it seemed I was invisible. Perhaps it was the decade old clothes I wore, or my inert disposition to find work. Finally, I decided to walk around the park.

At the other end of it, a short pudgy faced young man smiled as I passed by him for the third time. He sat on a wooden bench with a book in his hand. I sat next to him and smiled. He returned the smile shyly and went back to his book. I inched closer. He ignored me. I moved even closer, this time with obvious and abrupt movements. His eyes moved swiftly from the page to me. I tried to smile seductively, tried to flirt with him without a word, but it was no use. I could feel every one of my moves awkward and forced. He noticed as well.

"What do you want?" he asked without preamble. I was taken completely by surprise and had nothing to answer.

"You don't speak?" he asked.

"I do," I said, now moving to the other side of the bench, "I just..."

"I'm not much to like so I know you must want something."

"I ah...I need to make some money," I finally said.

He closed his book, took a deep breath and said, "I have fifty dollars in my apartment."

"Where's your apartment?"

"Centro Habana."

Out of all the individuals I could've approached, I had to pick one that lived on the side of town I couldn't be seen in. But I needed the money. With fifty dollars I could go back to Margot, get a room and get some much needed rest to then keep working.

"Let's go," I said. We walked in silence to the bus stop.

For fifty dollars the short and pudgy young man, whose name I had not cared to ask, took me from behind as many as three or four times. He had incredible stamina and was not satisfied after seconds or thirds. He grunted and sweated, was careless, clumsy, and wanted it only in that one position. Finally, after the fourth time, he crumpled onto the side of the bed while I stood to clean myself.

"You are great," he said. "Can I see you again?"

As I buttoned my oversized shirt, I remembered one of Kassandra's many advices: Regulars are the best clients. Just learn what they like.

"Sure," I said, "but I need to go now." He handed the fifty dollar bill and took it back when I reached for it.

"You never told me your name."

"Brunet," I said, now somewhat concerned that he wouldn't pay me. I'd forgotten the most important rule to collect the money up front. But I continued dressing without letting him know.

"Brunet, I'd like to see you again tomorrow."

I wanted to say no, that I was busy, that I had other things to do. But I needed the money, and my options were few.

"You have another fifty dollars?"

"I can get them by tomorrow."

"Okay," I said, "what time tomorrow?"

We arranged to meet at the same time, same place the next day. I finished dressing, took the fifty, kissed his fat cheek, and walked out.

The next couple of days went pretty quickly. With the first fifty, I rented a room back at the motel, got some cheap but sexier clothes, and bought some overpriced canned food. With the next fifty from Manuel —he had told me his name during our second meeting— I took a cab to Padrino's house. No one answered the door.

Now I had a little less than forty dollars and no prospects for the night. The cab dropped me off in front of the motel. I went in my room without looking at anyone and slept the entire night and most of the next morning. Margot woke me with a loud knock right before lunch time.

"There were some cops downstairs looking for you," she said nervously when I opened the door. "I told them I didn't know you, and there was no one staying here that fit the description they gave."

"What did they want?" I asked signaling for her to come in and closing the door behind her.

"I don't know. They said they needed to ask you some questions. You have to get out of here in case they come back."

"I don't have enough money for another room."

"My friend works at a hostel in La Habana Vieja. I can see if she has room for you. Why are they looking for you?" she asked carefully.

"It's a long story, but just know they're not good cops."

"Umph..." she scoffed, "what cop is in this city?"

"They get paid by my friend's chulo. He wants me to work for him but I refuse."

"Good for you. Don't let anyone exploit you."

I was surprised at her candid attitude regarding my profession, and I wanted to share more with her, to tell her how I really felt, to have her hug me and say things were going to be fine, to have her motherly protection. But she wasn't my mother, and I couldn't expect her to act like it.

"I can't offer my home, I live with my in-laws and their two other sons and wives. It is already too crowded for us. But no one will look for you at a hostel for tourists. You'll be safe there."

I wasn't sure about the safety issue anywhere, but

was grateful for the information, and the help. I packed my scarce belongings in a paper bag, and walked out with Margot. In the lobby, she instructed me to wait behind the counter by the wooden ladder. Within seconds, she was back with money in her hand.

"If you were never here," she said putting the money in my hand, "this room was never rented."

I didn't have any words to show my gratitude. I tried to give her the money back, but she wouldn't even hear of it. I squeezed her tightly, remembering how my mother used to hug me when she'd come back from one of her trips. There was little time for sentimentalities, she said, I needed to just go out the back door, get on the first cab to the other side of La Habana where her friend's hostel was. She told me the name of the street, the name of the hostel and her friend's name was Ana Maria. Any cab driver would know exactly where it was.

Twenty minutes later, I stood in front of a two-story building with a tricolor façade. The top part was a dark green, the middle a heavy brown, and the bottom part was beige. It seemed the building had stood for at least a century with its churchlike architectural design. Like the rest of the structures in the city, it was in the eternal process of reconstructive design, and its skeleton--nothing more than a few steel columns on wooden crutches--was exposed in the front only to be covered by thin Sheetrock in the back. For a moment, I thought it dangerous to enter the building as it might collapse at any minute. But the fear of death by the rubble was less present than being found by the cops or Camacho.

At the entrance, a woman with bleached blonde hair smoked a cigarette and leaned on one of the columns. She gave me an inquisitive look while she took a deep drag. I walked reluctantly toward her and smiled. She did not return the smile, but continued to inhale without taking her eyes off me.

"Buenas tardes," I said politely. "Do you have any rooms available?"

"This is a hostel. We have beds." She inhaled as she spoke.

Hostel so close to hotel. "Do you have any available beds?"

"They are only for tourists."

I walked up closer to her, paper bag in one hand, cash in the other. "Margot said you could help me."

The expression on her face did not change. She only inhaled deeply again, threw the end of the cigarette on the sidewalk, and stepped on it, then motioned for me to follow her into a generously proportioned room with single beds only few feet away from each other. It smelled muggy, and the stench of cigarettes was pervasive throughout. The floor was clean, the beds were made, and at the far end corner there was one person still in bed.

"He's sick," the woman said pointing her chin at the occupied bed. "Ate too much pork. Usually they're all out by ten. For Cubans it's forty pesos a night." She stopped in the middle on the large room. "You'll have a bed every night you pay for in advance. You don't pay in advance, you might not get a bed."

She now examined my face. I felt her stare but kept my eyes on the "amenities." There was a clothes line running across the back of the room, the showers were outside, three toilets inside, everything had to be shared, she explained. I needed a place to sleep, to rest so I could care less where or with whom at this point as long as it wasn't a jail cell.

I gave her the money, which was enough to cover two nights. I still had cash from Manuel's fifty, but it would not get me much. The woman turned and left me beside one of the beds. She said I could take that bed right there as she walked away. I put my bag on it and sat to think for a second. I could start walking the streets as early as now, but this part of the city wasn't populated by tourists. The majority of foreigners who stayed at the hostel were college students; the other occupants were destitute Cubans like myself, who could not afford anything better.

Resting my head on my hands and knees, I thought out my next move. I could go back to Manuel's apartment, tell him how much I "really" liked him, make another quick fifty, and get out. But it was awkward for a prostitute to show up at any man's door asking to see him. Usually it went the other way. I could wait until night, go on the hunt for a lonely soul, a desperate local, a drunken gambler. But I'd be wasting the day away sitting on that bed. The luxury of time was one of the many I did not possess.

I wished that at one point during our many conversations about leaving the island, Kassandra and I had discussed the name of the man who would've taken us to Miami. She had mentioned all the details: the size of the small boat, the need to take water jugs and sun block, milk for Kristen, cloth diapers, no space for spare clothes for us, all except the guy's name. With a name and what he did, it would be easier to find him.

Everyone in La Habana wanted to leave for a better life. Whether it was to Miami--first choice destination-- or to any other country, every Cuban wanted to leave. Of this, my mother always told me, there was no question. But not all the Cubans were willing to risk their lives or the little bit they did have. The chances of making it to freedom were always slim; you could drown, you could get caught in international waters and sent back, which meant you'd be spending the rest of your days in jail, your raft or boat could end up in the wrong country. The more desperate and younger people were willing to risk it all, but older people and people with young children were more reluctant.

Sunlight filtered through several wooden planks that reinforced the skeleton of a window behind me. Suddenly the sunlight was blocked, and as I looked at the woman who approached, it dawned on me that if anyone could help me, she was the one to talk to.

"You want work?" she asked standing directly in front of me, feet shoulder width apart, and looking down at my face.

"What do you mean?" I asked.

"Work? Money? You want to make money?"

"What kind of work?"

"The kind you do."

I stood to face her. She looked me in the eye with all the confidence I apparently did not have.

"You give me ten percent to find you clients, and we'll make good money together. On this side of town, there's no malecon, and not many tourists."

"Ten percent?"

"Ten percent. I'll never beat you, and I find rich clients." Taking a step back she reached into her bra to take out a pack of cigarettes and a tiny lighter. She examined me as she lit one.

I remembered Kassandra's advice to never have a pimp. But a pimp took all the money, and he beat you, and you had to have sex with him whenever he wanted to. This woman was not proposing to be my pimp, but a business partner of sorts. I was skeptical about the whole thing.

"How do you find rich clients?" I asked, naively thinking it was a valid question.

"That's my business. You want in or not?"

"I ah...can I think about it?"

"Think about it?" she said. "You go ahead and think about it all you want. I'm sure I can find twenty of you out in the malecon." She turned quickly on her heel and was out of sight leaving me with the smoke from the cigarette making circles in the sunlight that escaped through the planks. A woman pimp was better than Camacho, I supposed, and very quickly realized this was yet another opportunity from Yemaya. I ran after her.

The first client Ana Maria got for me was an old

man with wrinkles so deep in his skin they looked like small cuts. He was a Cuban who had left to Miami in the late sixties and came back every now and then to "enjoy the island." He didn't want to talk or fuck, which was great for me, but he wanted me to stick a plastic penis into his anus as I massaged his testicles and he jerked off. I was completely disgusted when he had an orgasm and a long trail of excrement oozed as I pulled out the ten inch long vibrator. But he paid $100 dollars and it took less than an hour.

At the hostel, I gave Ana Maria a $10, ran outside to shower, put the same clothes on and within another thirty minutes she was back smiling.

"You did good," she said. "He wants you back tomorrow."

I wanted to tell her I didn't want to do it, that I was so disgusted with the old man that I'd throw up if I ever did that again. But a $100 dollars in less than forty-five minutes was more than most of the jineteras got, and right now was not the moment for me to be picky about clients. I thought about my friend, who had never had the choice of saying yes or no to her pimp. I couldn't throw away the opportunity to make money to find a way out for her and the baby, but most of all for me. If I had at least a thousand dollars, I could reserve a space on a boat even if leaving the island would be more than five or six months ahead.

After two additional visits with the scarred old man, my second client from Ana Maria was more "normal." He was in his fifties, from some country in Africa I couldn't pronounce the name of, and all he wanted was sex in the missionary position and to spoon me afterwards. I took a light nap while he spooned me. Then I gathered my fifty dollars, told him it had been great and walked out of the cheap motel.

Within the first five days, I made close to $400 dollars. Ana Maria was proud. She said I was a good worker and that she had not yet gotten any bad comments about my performance. I was working nonstop; at least three clients a day. Not all the customers could pay a hundred dollars, but she never went under fifty in her negotiations, which was perfect for me because I was not good at negotiating. I was able to buy some new clothes and some shoes, and the rest I put away in a tree hole in the back of the hostel.

By the end of the second week, I told her I needed a day off to resolve some paperwork I had received from Miami. I had kept her thinking I'd soon be leaving so she was nicer to me.

I took a bus to a distant part of La Habana Vieja, walked two blocks from the last bus stop to the Padrino's house and waited in the corner. Within minutes, the old black Mercedes stopped in front of the house; Padrino got out from the passenger seat followed by Camacho and Kassandra who came out the back seat. She looked even thinner than when I had left her in the hospital, and her face, partly covered by a blue bandana, was of a bluish hue that spelled a beating. She was not carrying Kristen; no one was. I wondered what had happened to the baby.

I imagined Camacho had beaten the crap out of Kassandra as soon as she had been dismissed from the hospital. Her shoulders sunk in, she walked slowly, looking at the floor, and her neck was covered by a scarf probably to hide the attempted strangulation marks. I wanted to jump out and scream for her, grab her hand and make her run away with me, but I knew it was not the smartest thing to do in front of Padrino's house. So I waited.

A few minutes later, Padrino and Camacho walked out and jumped back in the car. As they sped away, I crossed the street and stopped at the door to the house. I was hesitant to knock. What if the old lady did not let me in? I knocked. Waited. Knocked again. Waited some more. I looked up at the windows that I thought could've been the ones in Kassandra's room and saw a silhouette. I knocked again. This time so hard, the skin on my knuckles peeled off a bit.

As the door creaked open, I could hear Kassandra yelling she'd had it, and when her face showed through the small crevice, my heart sank in. Now without any covers, I could see all the damage Camacho had done. Her lower lip was cut right down the middle while the upper one was so swollen, it sat tightly under her nostrils. Both of her eyes were blue-black, and on her right cheekbone there were two parallel sutures of at least an inch each. She swallowed a breath in fear, looked behind her, then stuck her head out to look both ways, and pulled me inside the house. She signaled silence with her index finger as I followed her up the stairs in the courtyard. In her room, she closed the blinds, locked the door behind me, and turned on her radio.

"What are you doing here?" she asked.

"I came to visit Camacho. What do you think?"

She smiled, tears filled her eyes. I hugged her tightly. She was too weak to give back the same energy.

"Did he do all this?" I asked releasing her from the hug and placing my hand on her jaw line.

"What do you think?" she responded with the same sarcasm I had just given her.

"Let's go, let's get out of here. I got this gig which is pretty good. When you heal you can work with me and we'll be out of here in a couple of months."

She turned to give me her back. "I can't go anywhere. They got Kristen."

"They who? Where is she?" I said approaching closer so she had no choice but to turn to face me again.

"She's still in the hospital. The day after the incident with you, the nurse came in with a piece of paper which says he's the father and he has custody of her. The doctor came in after and said I would not be released unless I signed it."

She turned her back to me again, her shoulders drooped, and I could sense her sadness without having to look at her eyes.

"Camacho told me he would kill her if I didn't."

"Kill her? She's in the hospital!"

"I know he had that doctor paid; I know what he's capable of."

"You have to go to the police."

"Have you not learned anything in the last few

weeks? I can't go to the cops; almost all of them are on Camacho's payroll."

"Then we just take her from the hospital. You are her mother!"

"With no legal rights to her. She has his last name now."

"But it isn't even his baby!"

"He knows that's the only thing that will keep me near him. Plus he looks at it as an investment. In twelve years she can start working."

"Not if I can help it," I said angrily pacing back and forth in the small bedroom. "We're going to get out."

"I lost my faith in Chango. She's supposed to be the saint that saves all those who are kept against their wishes, like she was. No matter how much I pray to her, she does nothing for me. And now she took my little girl."

"Santa Barbara didn't take your little girl. Camacho did," I said pushing down one of the blinds to get a better look outside. "Why don't you pack some stuff and come with me to the hospital."

"And what? They won't even let me be alone with her in a room."

"We'll find a way. Let's get out of here." But as soon as I said that and looked at her eyes, I knew my friend had given up her fight. I could feel the powerful sadness that had surrounded her for so long and that had finally won over her spirit.

With her shoulders still sagging and her stare adrift, she said, "I can't go anywhere, but you go. You write me from Miami and send me a few dollars every now and then."

"Kassandra," I said inhaling deeply and getting closer to her face, "I don't know as many people as you do. I don't even know anyone who knows anyone who owns a boat. We'll work at night. You stay at the hostel with the baby during the day, and I'll figure things out. When we have the money, we'll get out of here."

"Camacho will kill us both, and then what will happen to my baby?"

"We'll be okay. Camacho won't find you. He won't even bother looking for you because he'll think you left."

With a pitiful smile, she turned her back to me and slowly started to undress. Her shoulders blades were of a yellowish/greenish color that did not look healthy. In the middle of her back was a bruise that protruded horrifically, like a dirty tennis ball. As she turned slowly, her ribs revealed several long bruises in the shape of a shoe. He had kicked her while she was down, typical of him.

Most importantly, Camacho had succeeded in destroying her soul, her energy and her free spirit. I felt so much hatred for him. I wanted him to suffer, to live in pain for the rest of his days, to die an agonizing death alone. But it wasn't enough to wish all these things upon him. I couldn't live the rest of my life knowing that he would never pay for all the things he did to her, to me and God knows to how many other women. I vowed to seek vengeance, to make him pay. I just didn't know how.

My friend now stood facing me, smile gone, eyes blank, her body a contortion of bones, skin and bruises. Her small waist was covered with bruises and protrusions. Where there once were supple thighs, now only sagging skin. Where there once was a finely delineated young body, now stood in front of me a woman who had been so severely beaten her body shape had changed; her figure was so translucently distorted that I thought I was facing a middle-aged woman with a terminal disease.

"Look at me," she said solemnly, "how do you think I can make money looking like this?"

"I'll work. You just stay with Kristen until you heal. I'll figure it out for both of us, I told you already."

"How do we get Kristen?"

"Let's worry about getting out of here first."

"I can't leave anywhere without her. He'll kill her."

"He won't; he can't bribe the entire staff!"

Kassandra stood without flinching as if sooner rather than later I'd come up with a solution, an answer to all her problems. I thought I saw a thread of hope again; an abstract idea that I had somehow come into her life to save her and her daughter. Then she looked away. Instantly, I knew the whole thing was more me wanting to save her than her idea of me saving her. It was as if she had already given up on herself and was just waiting for me to do the same. But there was some hope. And that was all I needed.

"I don't know how we're going to do this, Kassandra. I don't have the first clue how to get

Kristen, or what to do after. But I know we'll figure it out. If I'm alone, and you're alone, Kristen has no one."

She faced the closed blinds now; her back to me, her hair partly covering some of the colorful spots of her shoulder blades.

"Why are you my friend?" she asked in a low whispering voice now putting her shirt back on. I had often thought about our friendship and how it had changed my life, how it had made me into someone I did not really like, how my mother would not approve of it. I took a deep breath.

"Because you need a friend right now."

"I always thought you became someone's friend because it benefitted you, not them."

"I don't know why you become someone's friend. But I know that I am yours and friends are there when you need them."

"You don't need me."

"I need you for everything. I need you to get out of here. I need you to teach me how to be a better jinetera so I can make the money to get out of here," at this I smiled and winked an eye. No smile back.

"The things that I can teach you are not good for you."

"You've taught me how to survive in this shitty city."

"You should've gotten training in another career. You're too smart to be a jinetera."

"Listen," I said approaching her, "I made a choice and I don't regret it. I would do it all over again if I had to." I lied.

"Really?" she said, now looking intently into my eyes to find the obvious untruth in my words. "You would become a prostitute and get involved with me knowing what kind of life I have? I sincerely doubt that."

"I could've walked away. I wasn't forced to stay."

"You really didn't have much of an option."

"There are always options. I could've gone back to my tia's house; I could've figured out a way to survive. I chose to do what I did. It's done now. Why are you questioning that?"

"I feel responsible for all that has happened to you. And now you want to help me get out of here, and get Kristen, and I just don't think I could do it."

"You're feeling sorry for yourself. Snap out of it." I had hoped the tone would get her to laugh or send me to hell. It did neither. She stood motionless, lifeless, like an empty cartridge you try to squeeze ink out of. She didn't smile, she didn't look at my eyes, she hardly breathed. It was the saddest I had felt her be.

I wanted to shake her and smack some sense into her. But I knew that would hurt her fragile state. For what seemed a long while, we just stood there without looking at each other, just feeling the sad energy between us. Then she slithered onto her bed, got into a fetal position, and closed her eyes. I sat on the edge of the bed. I was scared that Padrino or the old lady could just waltz in and catch me, but I saw the door was locked. Memories of the last few weeks replayed in my head. I lay down next to my friend to think of my next step.

The slamming of doors jolted me out of a deep sleep. Kassandra lay next to me, her arm around my waist, her leg intertwined with mine. I moved her slightly to see if she would wake up. No response at all from her. I pushed her arm off my waist, rescued my leg from hers and stood close to the door. I could hear voices, arguing voices, a man, and a woman? They were getting closer. I got up from the bed, looked around for a place to hide. There was an old fashioned wooden armoire in one of the corners, two night tables at each side of the bed, and a small table filled with religious offerings stood near the door. The voices were now closer, as if they were right outside the door. Then a loud knock threw me back a few paces.

"Kassandra, open the door." I recognized the old woman's voice.

"Are you okay, mijita?" Padrino's voice resonated throughout the room.

The handle on the door moved. I looked at my friend, who slept peacefully. I was a nervous wreck. I looked under the bed for a hiding spot. If they managed to come in, I had no doubt they'd have me kicked out at best. I slithered under the bed. I lay there listening to the commands to open the door, hoping Kassandra would wake up before they broke into the room. Minutes went by, and I felt no movement from the bed. She was sound asleep, and the voices kept getting louder. I waited. Then I heard footsteps walking away. I slid to the left side under the bed, got up and shook Kassandra's legs vigorously. She grunted, turned to the other side and kept on sleeping. She was not a deep sleeper; on the contrary, if you even coughed in the room while she slept, she'd wake up and could not go back to sleep. It was very strange that she could sleep through all this. I shook her legs again. No response.

I walked over to her side of the bed and noticed on the night table a small container of pills. There was no name on the container; neither of the patient or the medication in it. But this was not unusual. Medicine was so scarce that people often sold and bought it on the black market, and labels on containers seldom correlated with the actual medication inside. I opened the bottle to find only two triangular pink pills in it. I had no idea what they were for but immediately assumed Kassandra had taken the missing ones and that was why she wasn't getting up.

There was a half filled glass of water on the nightstand. I poured it on her neck. She turned, groaned, but still did not wake. Outside, I heard footsteps approaching again. This time I was sure they'd break through the door. I looked out the window. In front, the short apartment buildings and the solares next to them gave some shade to the house. The fall would probably kill me, but there was a ledge all around that could hold me for a few minutes, if I didn't look down.

I opened the window and climbed out. Just then, I could hear the door open and Padrino yelling at

Kassandra to wake up. My heart was pounding so loudly, I could hear it. My forehead was soaked with sweat, my palms trembled, and I could feel thick drops running down my spine, which was glued to the wall. I dared not look down. I knew my vertigo would get the best of me. I tried looking in to see what was going on but was afraid the six-inch ledge would give under my feet.

I stood still, barely breathing, just listening. The building in front of me was like the rest of the buildings in the city: dilapidated, ancient and still standing by the grace of hundreds of wooden planks nailed to its skeleton. The street below completely deserted. I took deep breaths, slow ones, focused on the walls across the street to keep from looking down. Then the voices inside the room got louder.

"What's the matter with her?" the old woman said.

"No se, no se," Padrino kept saying. "I'm trying to see if her heart's beating."

I was nervous about my precarious situation, but more worried about what might have happened to my friend. Seconds ago she had not been awake, but her heart was still beating. I wanted to run back in screaming to let her be, to put my ear close to her chest and listen, to make sure that huge muscle in her chest was pounding. Then I heard Kassandra's terrified screams. She was in agony, I could tell, and she kept repeating no, no, no, please don't. It seemed she was being forced to swallow something because her screams, off and on, were muffled grotesque sounds. Then a creepy silence followed by the shutting of a door. I waited a few minutes to make sure everyone was out of the room before climbing back in.

As I slipped back in through the window, I caught a whiff of something rotten in the air. Kassandra was lying on the bed face down, sobbing uncontrollably. I sat down next to her, ran my hand on her back but she didn't acknowledge my presence. She kept her face buried in the pillow and continued to cry. The rotten smell was now poignantly disgusting, and it took all my strength to not puke all over the bed.

"What is that smell?"

"You gotta leave before they find you, please." She said turning to look at me.

"I'm not going anywhere until you tell me what they did to you."

I felt her body tense up, almost as if she had stopped breathing while my breath became erratic again. Then she stood with her back to me, and walked towards the window I had left open. She turned to face me, smiled and mouthed "gracias" then turned and dove into the nothingness. I heard my own voice screaming no, but it was dreamlike, as if I was watching all this, and this scene could just be rewound, like the American movies of my childhood.

I ran to the window. Her body lay on the pavement, a leg grotesquely twisted and distorted, her face on top of a rapidly forming circle of blood. I kept screaming no and yelling her name between cries. The same feeling of desolation when I found out my mother had drowned now filled my entire being, and I knew that I was once again, all alone. This was not a movie.

Behind me, the half century old door sprang open. Padrino and the old woman stopped momentarily, then both ran to the window and looked down. The old lady cried out, Padrino immediately began to sob. They looked at me, at her body down on the street now surrounded by a few spectators.

"Did you do this to her?" Padrino asked me.

"Of course she did this to her!" the old woman yelled.

"I did not," I spat back at her. "You both did this to her," I continued, now pointing at the old man. "You were forcing something into her. You got her out of the hospital, and brought her here where you know she is not safe from that monster of your nephew!"

"How dare you?" the old lady yelled taking a couple of steps forward. "That is my only grandson!"

"Your grandson is the son of a bitch who did this to her." I had not yet finished the sentence, when I felt her hand smack across my face. I pictured myself grabbing the old woman's hair and pushing her entire body out the window my friend had just flown out of. But I quickly came to my senses and ran out of the room instead. They followed me.

On the street, I pushed some people in the crowd aside, took my friend's wobbling head and placed it on my lap. The scene in the hotel room just a few days before was replaying itself. I put my hand over her chest to feel a faint heartbeat.

"She's still alive!" I yelled. "Someone please call an ambulance!"

Padrino was standing behind me. The old woman

kneeled and began to pray in the language of *santeros*, a mixture of Spanish and the ancient Yoruba dialect. I looked down at my friend's bleeding head on my thighs. I tried to press where the blood was profusely coming out of, but the opening in her skull was bigger than my hand. Within seconds, I was covered in blood. The sticky fluid was beginning to coagulate in my thighs and hands. Kassandra's breath was shallow and the heartbeat was but a slight thump with seconds for intervals before the next beat. I looked around to see if anyone had called for help but no one had even moved. I screamed again for help. A young kid ran from the crowd yelling he would call the ambulance. Padrino stood still, like a marble figure, his face expressionless, painless. The old lady continued her prayers. I sobbed, held my friend, became aware that Camacho had joined the crowd and was already talking to cops. Then, from behind, someone yanked me from my friend's body, two men put her on a stretcher and into the mouth of an ambulance, and before I knew it, my hands were being cuffed and my head pushed into the back of a police car.

CHAPTER SIX

The stench of piss, shit and vomit lingered in the tiny cell and overtook my nostrils. I held my breath as long as I could, and then buried my face on the folds of my arms, took small breaths until my nostrils became acclimated to the disgusting odor. The walls had clear signs of mildew and decades of abandonment. I sat in the middle, where it was dry and there was no human waste, hugging my knees and resting my head on them. I knew this time there was no escaping out the back gate or a hidden door, and there was no one to run to for help.

The guard who had thrown me into the desecrated cell the day before, said I was being charged with first degree murder. I was petrified at the thought of spending the next twenty years in prison for the murder of my friend. I cried. Then I fell asleep on the cold cement floor.

When I woke up, a blue plastic tray with a bowl on it had been left by the side of the door. My body ached and I desperately needed to use the bathroom. I was also hungrier than I had ever been and realized that I had not had any food in twenty-four hours or more. I squatted in one of the corners to relieve myself, and then picked up the bowl that was filled with greasy water. I gulped the entire thing without a breath. My stomach still grumbled, my knees shivered as if they were in arctic water, my head was light. I felt about to collapse. Holding on to the wall, I inhaled the stench, breathed in deeply as I tried to regain my composure. My knees buckled, gave in, and I plopped down on the floor. I immediately started to cry again, out of desperation, out of helplessness again, out of God knows what plethora of emotions was running through my heart. My mother stood in front of me, guided by the faint light coming from the window so high up on the wall, I hadn't noticed it until now. Her face was solemn, gaunt, sad; her eyes on the verge of tears.

"I'm sorry I let you down, mami. I'm sorry that I'm not the daughter you would've wanted to have," I said sobbing at her feet, well aware now that it was only my mind, the memory of her that produced her image, and the certainty of her death pierced through me like Chango's sword did his enemies.

"I'm sorry that I've become someone you'd be ashamed of, that I didn't take your advice by not thinking about the consequences of my actions. I'm so sorry, mama." I could hear my own voice screaming now, yelling at the top of my lungs, crying uncontrollably. I felt her presence, her hand on my head, her forbearing energy reverberating through my body. Then I looked up. She smiled. Like always, her merciful and loving smile. I rested my head on the folds of my arms.

When I looked up, her image was gone, and only a sensation of peace was present. I felt a calmness I had not felt in a while, and I closed my eyes to envision the Great Mother Yemaya, the protector of the seas and women, whizing my mother away to heaven.

Just then the cell door opened, and a very tall woman dressed in what I could tell were expensive foreign clothes walked in. I thought I was having another hallucination, another piece of my mind that had become loose, the result of unyielding hunger.

"Get up," she said, "you're being released."

"Who are you?" I asked.

"Your guardian angel, courtesy of Mr. Brodstein."

"Mr. Who?" I said getting up now and wiping my clothes.

"Brodstein, Martin Brodstein, your business partner?"

I hadn't the slightest clue what was going on. I could only assume that this was a dream.

"My business partner?"

"Yes, isn't that what you said to the head of security at El Nacional?"

"I guess I did," I said.

"You don't want to discuss this in here. Let's go."

I followed her out the cave-like halls of the prison that were guarded by a few men in uniforms. Once on the street, a car waited for us. She gave the driver instructions to take us to El Nacional, turned to me and took a deep breath.

"I'm Mr. Brodstein's assistant. He's had me jump through hoops, not only to find you, but to get you out. So here's the deal. You are his prospective business partner. You have been out in the country side visiting a relative, but now you're back. You stick with your original story. "

"How...? What....?"

"Listen to me, and do so carefully. We got you a room at the hotel for the time being. We're going to get you some new clothes, and you are going to look the part."

"But I'm not really..."

"Uh uh, don't tell me anything. He asked me to find you, bring you back to him. That's what I did. I don't need to hear your story."

She was crude to the point of being rude. Her face, not pretty but not ugly either was more like a washboard, wooden planks that bore anything you put on them. Freckled, fair skin with dull blue eyes that did not release any emotions.

"Where's Martin?"

"He's in Canada today but will be back tomorrow to meet with you. Meanwhile, I'm supposed to get you ready."

"For what?"

"You are being charged with murder. Do you know that?"

"Yes," I said meekly, remembering the rude guard who had thrown me into the cell.

"I don't care if you did it or not. I'm not a lawyer. But I just paid a lot of money to get you out on bail. In a couple of weeks, you'll go in front of a judge and plead not guilty. Hopefully by then, Mr. Brodstein's legal team has arrived."

"Legal team? What does that mean?"

"That means you're going to have at least two

Canadian lawyers helping your public defender."

"I didn't kill my friend."

"I told you I don't care."

She lowered her window, took a deep breath of the air that rushed in, and turned to face me again.

"I'm sorry, I don't mean to be rude with you, but really, I don't like to get involved with Mr. Brodstein's personal affairs."

"So you know I'm not really his business partner?"

"I know what he tells me. He says you are his business partner, so you must be his business partner!"

I nodded slowly, understanding that even if she pretended not to care about anything that had to do with me, she felt enough empathy to be somewhat human. And that was more than I could ask of anyone I had just met.

The cab stopped in front of the hotel. An old man in a uniform opened the back door for us and we walked right into the lobby. The short pudgy manager immediately met us at the front desk.

"Ms. Davenport, what can I do for you today?" he asked her.

"Ah, good morning Raul, you can get Mr. Brodstein's associate here a nice room with some food in it. She's been traveling."

He gave me a look of disdain but said nothing. I smiled, a phony smile that let him know I didn't much care what he thought about me. He instructed his front desk attendant to do as Ms. Davenport wanted and walked away. The attendant, a young kid no more than eighteen, seemed nervous. Cubans were not allowed to stay in any of the hotels in the city. Of course with dollars, anything could be done in La Habana.

My guardian angel extended her hand to the kid. He took it, held it longer than usual, then went to a room in the back. He came back with a key, handed it to me, and courtly said enjoy your stay with us. In the elevator, I asked the woman what her name was. She said it was Helen, like Helen of Troy. I didn't know who she was referring to and didn't bother to ask. Helen walked me to the door of my room but did not come inside. She said to shower, eat something, and that she would be back in an hour to take me shopping.

In the eighties, public humiliations by the government were commonly done to those who opposed the Revolution and were known to be plotting to leave the island illegally. Another targeted group was people who like me now, made their living off tourists somehow. I was a little girl then, and these public stunts for the Revolution had died down considerably during this decade. But I remember one of the insults they'd hurl at women was- te vendes por un pitusa- you sell your soul for a pair of jeans. I knew what it meant literally back then. Now I understood why, because the first thing extranjeros want to do is feed and clothe you.

When I closed the door, I examined the room: one big bed, a table with two chairs, two night tables, and a balcony at the far end. I noticed there was no T.V., and no dresser with drawers like in other rooms I had seen. But I didn't have any clothes anyway. I had to get back to the hostel to pick up my few prized possessions from Ana Maria. But at the moment, all I really wanted was to shower and eat something. I was famished.

Within the hour, Helen was at my door. I wore the robe I had found behind the bathroom door because my clothes were smelly and dirty. She handed me a bundle of clothes, and a nice pair of shoes.

"The clothes are not mine. The shoes are but I don't know if they'll fit, I'm a size 37," she said.

"I use a 36, but these will be fine."

"Good," she said, "I'll wait for you downstairs." She turned and walked toward the elevator. I spread the outfit on the bed. It was a business suit a little too big for me, but it would do. My feet danced loosely inside the closed-toe shoes, so I took some toilet paper and stuck it in the front. Ten minutes and I was down in the lobby looking for Helen who was nowhere to be found. I took a seat in one of the comfortable couches, rested my head on the back, and dozed off. Next thing I knew, Helen was shaking my arm telling me we had to go. I got up with a jump and followed her outside to the car that had brought us.

The store was La Maison, the same one James had taken us to. The woman at the cash register recognized me. She smiled this time. Helen knew exactly where to look, what to pick, what to put together as an outfit. I followed her around the store like a little duckling following mama duck. I stayed close, listened and kept my mouth shut. She told the woman from the store that all this merchandise was to be charged to a credit card but that the owner of the credit card was not present. The woman said that would not be a problem.

A couple hours later, I was back in my room. There was a light knock and on the other side a voice said room service. On the cart there was ham and cheese and fruit and rice and vegetables and even bottles of water, and juice and things I didn't even know the names of. I stared at the tray filled with all these things to eat. How can there be so much need, hunger, lack of essential necessities for a people when outsiders got to enjoy the best the country had to offer?

In my sixteen years of life, I had tasted an apple once, drank bottled water only when my mother would bring them from other countries, and had devoured bars of chocolate because my neighbour would give them to me when we were done having sex. But meat, chicken, rice and beans were all strictly rationed, and depending how many people were in your family, you got enough to last you maybe two weeks, if you were very frugal. Most people lived on a meager diet of white rice and teaspoons of beans. The meat and chicken, when it was available, was left for the children, just like the milk, when there was some, it was saved for the kids whose teeth were still coming out.

I took a bite of the ham with a slice of cheese on top. It was delicious. I gulped some of the juice, and after licking one to see what it tasted like, I stuffed some strawberries in my mouth. I thought they would soon come back to pick up the tray and I had to eat as much I could before that happened. I thought about Kassandra, and how she might or might not have had the opportunity to taste these things with James; I wasn't sure. But I was sure that if I didn't do anything for Kristen, she'd end up the same.

Hours later, the ringing phone on the bedside table woke me. The clock on the wall said it was four o'clock in the afternoon.

"Hello?" I said into the receiver.

"Milena, it's Helen. I need you to come down to the lobby. You got ten minutes, okay?"

"Okay," I said still somewhat asleep. I put the receiver back in the cradle and put my head back on the pillow.

Thoughts of Kassandra and of Kristen filled my head again. Memories of my mother, of Martin Brodstein. Now I knew his full name. I wondered why he wanted to help me. The restaurant idea had popped in my head just to save my skin. He could've found out through Helen, but she wasn't giving out any information. I wondered if there was some ulterior motive for him to help me. What could an orphaned underage jinetera offer this man who seemed to have everything?

I thought about the last week since I had been with him. Had I not gone to the hospital to see Kassandra that day, perhaps now she would be alive and enjoying the good luck Yemaya had bestowed upon me. The phone rang again.

"Are you ready?" Helen asked from the other line.

"Not yet," I said trying to recover my quivering voice.

"Hurry up, I called you twenty minutes ago!"

I'd been crying for twenty minutes? I jumped off the bed, threw on one of the fancy new outfits: a light pink pleated skirt with a sophisticated white blouse that had a kerchief hanging on the front, and one of the two pairs of shoes Helen had picked out for me. I ran out of the room and once the elevator L button lit up, I remembered I had left the key on the bedside table.

In the lobby, Helen was talking to the head of security, the man who had tried to make me confess to being a jinetera, and who had almost broken down had it not been for the manager who had walked in. He was clearly surprised to see me.

"This is Mr. Brodstein's partner," Helen said pointing at me. She gave him the same relative in the countryside story she had given the manager. He listened intently, put his hand out to shake mine without taking his eyes off me. I shook it, smiled politely, and followed Helen outside.

It was warm and muggy, and from the streets came this foul odor of rotting food. This was the usual in La Habana; seldom, a breeze from the ocean blew by.

"There's this little place I've been looking at for your business," Helen said stopping right outside the door. "We're going to take a ride there and you let me know what you think," she said casually, as if this was just another business meeting for her.

What I thought about what? What business? Was she kidding me? "What do you mean my business?"

"Your restaurant? The one you're going to open up?"

"But that was just..."

"I told you I don't want to hear your story. Brodstein told me you and him were opening up a restaurant in La Habana and that I needed to find a good location for it."

"I don't even know how to cook," I confessed.

"Good to know. I won't be one of your first customers."

An old beige Cadillac pulled up and Helen walked toward it. The air was humid, dirty, hot, and I was already sweating. We got into the old car where it was crisp. She told the driver to go to El Vedado, a part of the city where only people who had families in the US lived because their families sent them dollars every month, and with dollars, you could live in the nicest parts of La Habana.

The cab took some short cuts and turned on streets I didn't know. Helen was not very talkative. She had taken out some papers from a briefcase that was already in the back of the car and had begun to read them. The car kept turning onto unfamiliar streets. The houses in this neighbourhood were in better shape than anywhere else La Habana. They stood on their own —no wooden bones to aid their skeletons— and the paint wasn't peeling off. The streets were cleaner than those in the malecon, but they were littered with people walking about, standing in long lines, sitting on portable chairs. For a second, I wondered what was going on, and then quickly realized it was the beginning of August when the rationed goods were distributed. I remembered when my mother and I stood in long lines for soap, the cheap kind that made your skin breakout, for rice, for milk and if we were lucky, for canned meat that had been imported from some eastern European nation.

"Do you have any form of identification with you?" Helen asked without taking her eyes off the papers.

"No," I said.

"Where's your libreta?"

"Don't know, my aunt says my mother took it with her."

"You have an aunt?"

Had I given out information I shouldn't have? "Yea, she's my mother's half sister."

"So you do have some family?"

"I don't consider her family anymore."

"Why not?"

I didn't know how to answer this question. My aunt had been the only one who had taken care of me when my mother died, yes, but I was also certain she had been the one to take the jewelry my mom had left me, and my libreta was probably how she got extra milk and rice for the kids.

"I don't get along with her," I said.

"Ok, well, you know you're going to need to show your papers."

"I don't have any."

"What hospital were you born in?"

"La Covadonga," I said.

"You need to go there, have them give you a copy of your birth certificate and take it to the city for them to put the stamp on it that makes it legal, and you're good to go."

I had to somehow tell her that I was not nineteen, but that in less than a month, I'd be seventeen. And that information, I knew, would make a huge difference in the way things worked out for me, or not. I had lied to Martin, I had lied to Helen, the very people that were now trying to save me from spending the rest of my life in a Cuban prison.

"Helen," I said as the car made a sharp right turn, "I have to tell you something."

"Uh oh, told you don't want to hear your story."

"It's not my story. It's my age."

Now she looked up from her papers, pen in hand, squinting to get a better look at my face. I looked down, hands fidgeting, my feet pidgin toed.

"I'll be seventeen in two weeks," I said in a low voice.

"Does Brodstein know?"

I said no. Helen pushed the papers to the right side, released the pen, breathed in deeply and exhaled slowly. I didn't dare take my eyes off my shoes.

"That's why you don't want to show me your papers, huh?"

"No, I really just don't have them." I told her what had probably happened to them..

"Okay," she said, "we have to take care of that before we do anything else. You know I'm gonna have to tell Martin."

I nodded taking notice it was the first time she had called him by his first name.

"And I don't think this will sit right with him. I mean it changes everything; you know the legal age for anything in Cuba is eighteen." I nodded again, kept my eyes on my shoes, too embarrassed to look at her.

She turned to the driver, gave him instructions to go back to the hotel, grabbed her papers and started reading again. She didn't say one more word to me. In the lobby, she pressed the elevator button. Once inside, she said curtly: "Don't tell anyone, don't talk to anyone, don't come out of your room unless I call you." And with that advice, the elevator door closed.

After waiting a while for the front desk to give me a spare key to my room, I started undressing as soon as I was in it. How would Martin take the news? Would he still want to help me? I thought what Kassandra would do in my case. What was Helen going to do now about the restaurant plans? I had so many questions that were to remain unanswered. But the most pressing was whether to remain here or to leave, back to the motel, back to the streets I didn't yet know how to work, back to Manuel, to Ana Maria's clients, to sleeping on a cot, to being hungry all the time.

It was close to six now- stomach grumbling- I went down to the lobby. Immediately, I knew I shouldn't have disobeyed Helen. The manager approached me as soon as I walked out of the elevator and asked where I was going.

"To get some food," I said despondently.

"There's room service, you know."

"I needed to get out of my room."

"You really shouldn't have."

"Am I being kept a prisoner in my room? I wasn't informed."

"You got a smart mouth on you."

"Yes, my mother taught me well," I said and walked toward the restaurant on the far corner of the lobby.

At the bar, I asked for a Coke. The bartender looked at me quizzically as if my asking for an American drink made me into a veritable traitor, but he served my drink and continued with his work. There was a man slumped over the bar, two empty shot glasses in front of him, cigarette dangling from the corner of his lips. I squinted to get a better look at him. He turned his head just a bit letting the bar light shine on his cheek revealing a familiar face. James. My first client. I looked away quickly, hoping he was too drunk to recognize me. I took my Coke, walked to the other end of the bar, and sat with my back to him. If he recognized me, he would surely make a big commotion about it and would most likely want me to come up to his room. Out of all the hotels in La Habana, he had to end up at the one I was in. I didn't finish my Coke. I started to walk slowly toward the door when the bartender called out for me.

"Oye, bonita, you have to pay for that Coke," he said.

"I don't have any cash," I said.

"Room number?" he asked.

I told him, he winked giving me permission to leave. I walked out of there hurriedly. The manager, who stood behind the front desk, stared at me as I made my way from the door of the bar all the way to the elevator, a direction I briefly contemplated against. I felt self-conscious, heavy with my walk, as if I had committed the worst crime and was only delaying the inevitable sentencing for it.

The banging on the door made me jump out of a deep sleep. The sun shone brightly in my sleepy eyes. I rushed to the door to see Helen standing with a cup of coffee in her hand, wearing a gray suit and red shoes that were sure to be more expensive than anything I'd ever owned.

"Let's go," she commanded. "Martin's plane will be here in less than an hour and we still have to see about your papers."

"My papers?" I asked groggily.

"I spoke to him yesterday. He gave me specific instructions to get your papers in order."

"You told him?"

"Only that you didn't have any identification."

She met my eyes for a split second and even though I couldn't pinpoint the emotion she felt, I was all gratitude. I knew sooner rather than later I would have to tell Martin; not just about my age, but the whole story of Kassandra and Camacho, and little baby

Kristen.

"Thank you," I said, walking back toward the bathroom. Helen just stood at the door. "Come in," I said, "I'm going to get dressed. I'll be just a minute."

She walked in somewhat reluctantly, cup of coffee to lips while examining the contents of the room. She didn't close the door behind her, and only walked into the front part of the room. I chose some black pants and a silk purple blouse she had picked for me at the Tourists Only store.

"Purple suits you," she said.

"San Lazaro was one of my mother's favorite saints," I said, unaware that by saying this, I was assuming she knew about the melee between Catholicism and the Yoruba religions.

"I'm not Cuban, so I wouldn't know."

"Where are you from?" I asked her while getting dressed.

"Born in Canada, American dad, French mom."

Her answer left room for more questions, but I left it at that. I put my shoes on, and we walked out. The same Cadillac waited for us at the door to the hotel. We jumped in. This time she didn't have any papers to read, no briefcase, only a small red purse that matched perfectly with her shoes.

She instructed the driver to go to La Covadonga Medical, in Guanabacoa; still part of the greater La Habana area, but a good twenty minutes away. Helen stared out the window, thinking.

"If you want me to help you, you need to shut your mouth, and follow my lead, okay?" She said slowly and clearly. "I have a contact at the Ministry of Census. I made a phone call yesterday, and she gave me a name at the hospital, a woman who's going to help us."

I kept nodding, unsure if I should ask any questions. I had a thousand of them whirling in my head, but I could tell she wouldn't counsel me on personal things. She was matter of fact about everything and had not mentioned a word about what I did for a living, although I was sure she knew.

"You are going to say your story, just like you told me, except your date of birth will be in 1974 instead of 1976."

"Right."

"We need to get you new papers, so we might as well just kill two birds with one stone."

"Isn't that illegal?"

She stared at me, a deep long stare that could peel off layers of skin. "I don't think you've been worried about being on the right side of the law lately."

"Not for me, but for Martin."

"Don't worry about that now."

"Wouldn't the hospital records show the correct year?"

"That's what we'll pay to change."

I nodded in agreement knowing how important it was to have dollars in your pocket, especially when you were breaking the law.

"I don't have any money to pay her with."

"I know. Brodstein's paying."

I had learned that no one did anything without

wanting something back. Why had he taken all this interest in me after just one night? I was sure he'd had other jineteras before, just as young and pretty as me, maybe with more experience, which was a plus in my business. So I couldn't figure it out.

"You'll have your chance to ask him today," Helen said reading my expression.

I gave her a faint smile still amazed at how she always seemed to know. I looked at her freckled face, at the lines around her eyes, at her hands, which had clear signs of at least four decades of life.

"I'm a lot older than I look," she said without taking her eyes off the window. "Believe me when I tell you I could be your mother."

My mother had looked quite young for her age, too. Her body had had no signs of the proverbial age weight gain, she had the legs of a twenty-year-old ballet dancer, the skin of a teenager sans the acne, and with her hair always pulled back, there was no way anyone could tell she was thirty-six. But she used to tell me that your thirties were not like your twenties; things happened to your body you were completely unaware of only a decade before. My own body had gone through a lot in only two weeks, and it felt tired, dirty, different.

"I wish my mother was still alive," I said thinking out loud.

"I'm sorry," she said.

Though she didn't ask, I told her how my mom had thought about leaving for months. Her last attempt taking her life, giving me a new one, turned inside out.

"And that's why I decided to..."

"You don't have to tell me," she said, winking an eye.

Helen didn't let me confess to being a jinetera. She really didn't care what I had done. She didn't judge me for my decisions, she got paid to help me. "Helen," I said shyly, "would you help me with anything I ask?"

"Depends. Brodstein only pays me to take care of the things he wants, not what you want."

"Okay," I said. If things worked out, I'd be able to somehow help Kristen, but I had to first help myself. I didn't say anything else the rest of the way to the medical center. Once the car pulled up in front of it, Helen took out a small plastic badge from her purse. She pinned it to the right side of her lapel. I looked closely at it. Medical Records Auditor.

"I am very resourceful, I told you. Keep quiet and we'll be all right." I nodded as she walked on in front of me.

The conditions in this hospital were not any better than they were at the city hospital although the equipment seemed to be about a decade newer, which still made it around twenty years old. This hospital was cleaner though, and the people in it seemed nicer, happier; some even smiled as they passed me by.

I followed Helen into a maze of corridors that led to the records office where a woman with bright orange hair sat in front of a square hole that had been cut into the wall. She smiled politely when she saw Helen, and a buzzer immediately went off. Helen walked in through the buzzing door. I followed into a smaller version of a maze, this one with ceiling high filing cabinets in rows; each row named with a letter. Helen didn't stop at any of them but walked on into the back of the gigantic room where a lone desk was unoccupied. She looked around, called out a hello, waited a few seconds, and then sat behind the desk. She proceeded to open the drawer in the middle and take out a stack of index cards.

"Pull up that chair," she instructed me pointing to a chair by the side of the desk. She then parted the index cards down the middle, handed them to me and said, "See if your name is on any of these."

I looked at each card carefully, slowly, repeating in my head the name printed on it. Below each name, a date, and a letter, which Helen said was the corresponding letter to the filing cabinet where all of that person's information was. I thought, we could be here forever. But then realized that the year on all the cards was the same. 1976. I assumed Helen had called ahead to have the cards from 1976 ready. They were not in alphabetical order and there had to be at least a couple thousand of them. After a few minutes, I was losing hope. What if my father had had someone destroy my card so that there would be no proof of my birth? My father had sent my mother away to have me, but as soon as she had come back into the city, she had registered me in this hospital. I didn't think that was the same as having been born in the hospital. I let Helen know about this minute but important detail.

"It doesn't matter where you were actually born. If

she registered you here, your card's gotta be here."

So we kept on looking. I looked up at the round clock on the wall. A half hour had now passed and I remembered Helen saying we would have to pick Martin up at the airport.

"Don't we have to get Martin?"

"We'll make it. Keep looking."

As I passed one card to the back of the pile in my right hand, my name came into clear view on the next one.

"I got it," I said, "I found my card!" The letter C was right under my name.

Helen snatched the card from my fingers. She stood and walked to the six feet high file cabinets. I followed her, my heart pounding. My mother had always been rather short in details about her experience with my father. I never knew much about him until he defected to Miami. Then, through the neighbors, I found out about all the things he had done to my mother once she had given birth to me. He had never wanted anything to do with me legally. So two weeks after I was born, my mother applied for a new birth certificate giving me her own last name.

Helen grabbed two files from the top cabinet. She was at least as tall as Martin, and he was at least as tall as the cabinets. She handed the files to me, pointed back to the desk. I sat and opened the first one. It had all of my mother's information; her mother's name, her father's, where she was born, all the pertinent details of her birth. The other file was mine. Pretty much same info except for my father's part. It was all blank. Not even a name. Helen sat back in the chair, crossed her arms in front of her chest, and tilted her head to look at me.

"You're not surprised all that info about your dad is blank?"

"I knew he didn't want it to be known I was his."

"Why not?"

"He was married. He was a revolutionary. My mother was always an antirevolutionary. From what I've heard, he was not stupid."

"You don't remember him?"

"Not at all. I never met him. He left for Miami and my mother never heard from him again."

It almost seemed as if she was going to hug me, but instead she took the files from my hand, opened the two prongs at the top, and took out my birth certificate. She opened the drawer and stuck it in there.

"Let's go get Martin," she said standing up.

On the way to the airport, Helen sat quietly next to me; her right cheek resting fully on her right palm. She stared at nothing. I was nervous about Martin knowing I had lied to him about my age. Scared about going back to jail for a very long time. I fidgeted and fixed my clothes every which way. I bit the inside of my cheeks, my mother's old habit when she was nervous and one that I had recently inherited. I felt the drops of sweat run down my spine to die at the intersection of my buttocks. Helen noticed.

"He's very understanding. Just tell him the truth this time."

"About everything?"

"Everything!" she said. "Just tell him everything that has happened to you."

I nodded, started to cry, out of nervousness perhaps, for my mother, for my dead friend, for the situation I had gotten myself in without thinking about the consequences. My mother always told me that for every move I made in my life, there'd be consequences, some good, some bad. I had not made a wise move since she had left, so there was no possibility of any good consequences for me. I felt lost.

"No good's gonna come from crying, little girl. Wipe them off and smile. Brodstein doesn't do drama."

I obediently ran the back of my hand under my eyes, straightened out my hair, fixed my clothes again. Helen didn't take her eyes off me.

"I know how it feels to be all alone in the world. You gotta hang on to the first good thing you get, and then you consider your options."

The first sentence now made perfect sense to me; here was the reason she was detached and cold even if her actions told otherwise. The second sentence was clear heartfelt advice. Helen cared.

"Thank you," I said. She simply nodded without taking her eyes off mine. I wanted to hug her, to close my eyes and feel as if her arms were my mothers'. The moment I inched closer to her, she turned her face and looked out the window. I took in some air, hoping that in breathing the icy chill that had suddenly come over her, I too could become indifferent to emotions at the clap of a finger.

CHAPTER SEVEN

From the back of the car, Martin looked older than I remembered him. In a beige guayabera, he reminded me of the old Cuban men who sat around at the park near my house and played dominos, drank rum and talked about Castro all day long. Helen got out of the car, waited at the foot of the stairs for Martin to walk down. In front and behind him were two men dressed in dark suits. I remembered when Kassandra and I picked up the two Americans; how she had fought one of them, how we had run out of that room with our shoes in our hands. I shook the bad memory off.

The driver inched the car closer to the plane, pressed a button that opened up the trunk. One of the men carried a small suitcase, the other a briefcase. Helen greeted Martin with a handshake, she immediately began talking. I wasn't sure what to do when he first got into the car. Should I hug him? Should I kiss his cheek? Should I just shake his hand like Helen had? One of the two men in suits opened the passenger door and Helen got in. She looked back and smiled. Martin talked briefly to the man who held the briefcase while the other one stuck the suitcase in the trunk. Then he got in the car holding the briefcase. He smiled politely, as he had done the first time we'd met, then he sat close to me and kissed my cheek lightly. I was so nervous, I couldn't even return the kiss, I just sat there frozen. The car took off, and as soon as it hit the road, Helen turned and started talking in English so fast I wasn't able to pick up one single word. Martin waved his hand in disdain, said a sentence out of which I understood the word "later". Helen immediately stopped talking, and turned to face the front. Martin put his arm around my shoulders and squeezed me. I was finally able to move and returned the squeeze.

"How are you?" he asked in his almost perfect Spanish.

"Bien," I said, "y tu?"

"Been in better health, but happy to see you again."

"You're not mad at me?"

"We'll discuss that later. Driver, take the fast way to the hotel, please. I'm tired."

The driver nodded and made a sharp right hand turn. No one said a word for the remainder of the ten-minute drive. Martin looked out the window and kept the squeeze on my shoulders. Helen played with an electronic tiny book that had its own little pen attached. I practiced in my head how I would explain the last two weeks to Martin.

At the hotel, he went straight to his own room, said he wanted to shower, for Helen and I to meet him in an hour to grab a bite. He kissed my cheek and walked into the elevator. Helen nodded, held me from going into the elevator with him.

"Is he always this dry?" I asked her.

"He is with me," she answered, signaling for me to follow her. She sat in one of the leather couches in the lobby. I had noticed the fancy furniture, but had not dared to sit on them in fear I might be asked to move.

"If I know him well enough, he will come through with his word and help you with your business venture."

"Helen, there's no business venture."

"Listen to me, you and him are going to open up a restaurant, that's what you need to get into your head."

"But...."

"But nothing. That's what's going to happen, and if you're as smart as I think you are, you are going to be the sweetest Cuban girl he's ever met in La Habana. You're going to tell him the truth about your life and who you are, and then just let the cards fall where they may."

"He knows what I am."

"Good, refresh his memory." And with that, she stood and walked to the elevator leaving me on the couch thinking.

Half hour later Martin was knocking on my door. When I opened, he walked in and looked around the room.

"I'm sorry I never came back that day. The manager didn't believe that I was with you, and he had me arrested," I started nervously.

"I know. But what happened to you after that?"

I sat on the edge of the bed, inhaled deeply and told him, without many of the gruesome details, about the last week.

"I know you think it is all a story but please believe me, it isn't."

"I believe you, I don't have much choice. Let's go get some food and talk about business. You can tell me the rest later."

The rest of the afternoon went pretty quickly with Martin and Helen talking about what the restaurant was going to look like, where it was going to be, what the name of it would be. I wanted to ask if they were serious about all the planning but since they talked so much about it, I figured it would have been a stupid question. I had come up with the lie of a restaurant to save my skin, but they talked as if it had been real from the beginning. Martin even asked Helen if she knew someone that could cook. She said she didn't but that wasn't hard to find at all. They talked about permits and papers and buying the supplies, about how to run the place, what kind of people they wanted to frequent and how they would get them there.

Their brains worked simultaneously, and when one thought of something, the other followed with a new idea, another concept. I admired the way Helen made things clear for Martin. She knew it all. All the people to pay in order to expedite matters, all the major foreign investors that had successful businesses in La Habana, and all the cops she needed to "take care of." When referring to this last group, she held up her curled fingers with the sign for quotes and winked my way. I knew then she understood my need for redemption and revenge, and she was willing to help.

But I still didn't know I fit into their plan.

Martin wasn't so thoughtful. He didn't look at me or her too much, kept his eyes on a notepad, pen in hand, scribbling one or two words of every other sentence said. It seemed such an odd thing to do for me, but he did it almost robot like, as if programmed to move very little, only the pen in constant motion being swiveled back and forth between thumb and forefinger when not writing. He was not particularly good looking, but he was tall, dressed well, impressive in his mannerisms. He walked the lobby as if he owned it, and talked to the staff as if he paid their measly salaries. Yet there was something about his eyes when he looked at mine that wasn't so tough, something that melted in him, and I knew why he wasn't looking straight at me in front of Helen.

Being with both of them was a bombardment of goodness in my life. I missed my mother more than ever, but if she had had it her way, this turn in my life would not have been such a bad option, given all I had done since she had died. I smiled. Martin noticed.

"You look happy?"

"I am. So happy that you two are in my life."

We were sitting at a restaurant in front of the water by the bay, near the ancient ruins of El Morro, a citadel that had been built back in the 1600's to protect the island from invaders. It was a French place, the menus were in French, the food was French, the servers, most of them French, only a few Cubans who cleaned the tables and floor. Martin spoke perfect French, or at least what sounded to me as perfect

French. Helen ordered everything in English. I spoke the only language I knew.

"This is more or less what I had in mind for our place," Martin said looking around. Helen looked around as well.

"But not the food," Martin continued, "I'd like the food to be a mixture of Cuban and Spanish; plus I don't want to compete with my friend."

"There are more Spanish restaurants on the island than they are French," Helen informed.

"Yes, but I don't know any that mixes in the traditional Cuban meals."

"We'd have to find someone that could cook Spanish food."

"Find her then," he replied.

The waiter brought us a beautifully decorated bottle that I assumed was wine, but when after showing it to Martin he ceremoniously popped the loud the cork, I knew it was champagne. I drank the first glass slowly, remembering what champagne had done to me that night at the club with Kassandra and James; the second glass went smoother, quicker. Not long after, the waiter brought out another bottle. It was a celebration, Martin said, a big celebration.

The city was coming alive in its darkness when we left the restaurant. There was a scheduled blackout that evening for four hours. As a way to conserve energy, the government scheduled these blackouts every week, sometimes twice or three times during one week. But when we drove by el malecon, the blackout didn't seem to affect the people there. Some were already beginning their evening work; jineteras and their pimps, dealers and their daily clients, vendors and their hustle. I shuddered at the memory of walking the bay wall, the two pigs, the night I attacked Camacho.

"Are you okay?" Martin asked me.

"A little dizzy," I said. "Champagne doesn't really agree with me."

"Champagne agrees with everyone; it's just that not everyone agrees with champagne," he said laughing. Helen laughed as well. I didn't really get the joke, but smiled as if I did. I felt light headed, confused about the signals Martin was giving me, and desperate to use the bathroom.

When we reached the hotel, I ran into the women's restroom while Martin and Helen went straight to the bar. On the wall, in front of the stalls was a square clock. It was ten o'clock. I was exhausted. My feet hurt in the fancy new shoes, my head wobbled with all the champagne in it. I wanted sleep.

But I dragged myself to the bar where Helen and Martin were having drinks. I felt a tinge of jealousy. Helen was so secured, sophisticated, knowledgeable. She was still taking notes in her little book. Although I could tell she was more relaxed than without the champagne, she was still in full control. I was not. My body was letting me know that it needed rest.

Martin looked at me and said, "You need to go up to your room. You look like hell."

"I told you champagne and I just don't get along," I said, trying too hard to be witty, like Helen. She smiled, patted my head like you would a good dog. I smiled back, ran my hand by where she had just run hers.

"We're going up," Martin said. "Charge everything to my room," he ordered Helen. "We'll talk in the morning."

Helen nodded, sipped her champagne, looked at her little book that had just lit up. Martin put his hand on my back and softly led me out towards the elevator. Inside it, I rested my head on his shoulder, complained about my stomach, about the dizziness. I thought Martin would want sex, and I'd have to comply since he was my savior, and I had no other way to repay him. But at the door to my room, he kissed my cheek, told me to sleep well; we have a full day ahead of us tomorrow, and left.

I plopped down on the bed thanking La Caridad del Cobre for her protection, Martin for his perceptiveness, Helen for her intelligence, and Kassandra, because had it not been for her, I'd still be eating rotten food and sleeping on a cot at my tia's. I didn't know how I was going to show her my gratitude, but I was sure her and my mother were looking down at me, cheering, thanking and praising Yemaya.

In the morning it was clear. I had to find Camacho. Find out what happened to Kristen. Ask Helen for guidance with all this.

The lobby, usually bustling with tourists and employees was quiet, empty. It was only seven in the morning. The last two days had been very different from the last two weeks, and I felt a different person now. I no longer walked the lobby in fear of the rude manager, or the security, or of any tourist recognizing me from el malecon.

"Perdón, señorita," a male voice said from behind me as I leafed El Granma and sipped my café con leche. I turned to find the head of security to the hotel pleasantly smiling.

"Can you come with me?" he asked.

"I'm not doing anything wrong this time, ask the manager. My room number is..."

"No please, I know, I know you are who you say you are. I just want to talk to you."

"Can't we just talk here?" I was sitting on the fancy couches. No longer fearsome, now they made me feel important.

"Okay, then, here's where is going to have to be. I want to beg your forgiveness."

"Forgiveness? Why?"

"Because my instinct told me you were telling the truth. I refused to listen. And I might have been the cause of unnecessary tears."

Tears? I thought. The last two weeks had been hell, and he thought I had just cried? He might have been the cause of my tears? Of course he was partially at fault, he knew I had been telling the truth, well not all the truth, but he knew I didn't fit the typical young jinetera description. He could tell I wasn't a veteran. And he still sent me to jail!

"You sent me to jail." I said calmly, not showing too much emotion, like Helen did when she wanted to intimidate someone.

"I didn't think..."

"You didn't think?" I felt a strong urge to yell, to spit at him, to hit him even, although I knew it would solve nothing other than to let him know how angry I was. But I took one good look at him and saw so much sadness that resembled my own, I could not bring myself to be spiteful and mean.

Instead, I said, "How could you not have known?" in a softer voice than I had anticipated.

"I thought I would have the chance to talk to you again. But when I came back, you were gone. And I never did anything to try to help you. Can you forgive me for that?"

"Why is it so important that I forgive you?" I asked, naturally curious about his persistence.

"My daughter, she was your age, maybe a year or so older. She became a jinetera to feed her son." A sudden uncomfortable silence now filled the space between our bodies. I looked up from the paper. Tears were stubbornly filling the white of his eyes.

"She took our grandson with her on a boat with fifty other people about six months ago. We haven't heard from them; the boat hasn't been found, and no one has contacted us about them."

"My mother drowned on a raft. You remember I told you?"

"That's why not helping you has eaten my conscience." He bowed his head in what I felt was truthful regret.

Redemption. Everybody's looking for it. Everybody needs it. For Cubans, the search for basic necessities often leads them to do things they wouldn't even think of doing under circumstances of no duress.

"If I help you, maybe someone out there in la yuma or wherever she is will help her and Willy."

"How old is Willy?"

"Ten months."

And there it was. The cause of a sadness so deep it oozed out of every pore in that man's body. If I gave him the chance for redemption, mine would be guaranteed, no? Plus, I really needed his help.

"You can help me find someone," I said after a long pause. "A little baby, about a month old."

"Yours?"

"No, a friend's. But now she's with some bad people that will make her into a jinetera as soon as she turns twelve."

"You need to find her, and take her, not just find her..."

"Exactly."

He nodded but seemed to get a little nervous.

"These people? They are foreigners?"

"No, *habaneros*."

"Members of the government?"

"Don't think so but in La Habana, you never know."

"You know you're gonna have to leave the city?"

"I know." Now I was nodding nervously.

"Do you have an address?"

"She might still be at the hospital."

"Name?"

"Kristen...Garcia," I said, remembering that

Camacho had given her his last name otherwise she would have been Kristen Martinez, the last name I would have had if my father had given it to me.

"Kristen is not a common name in La Habana; it shouldn't be difficult if she's still in the hospital."

"Here's the address if she's not in the hospital." I handed him a corner of the newspaper I had written the address on and ripped. "That's where you're going to find it difficult," I said accentuating the difficult, a technique I had heard Helen use many times, especially when hotel employees told her something couldn't be done.

"Children that age belong with their mother. I'll ask my friend who is a police man to come with me. We'll say her mother has claimed her in the police station and they have to give up the *criatura*."

"Her mother's dead."

"Where's the father?"

"The real one, who knows. The man whose last name Kristen has is the guy who beat up her mother, my friend who was murdered by his family."

I made it short and sweet for him; omitting the gruesome details while letting him know the whole truth about my situation.

"Now I feel worse than before. And to think I could've done something to help."

"'Don't feel bad anymore. You're helping me now. This has to be done quickly, and quietly."

He nodded. A complicated plan with too simple instruction was formulating in my head. I didn't yet know what I would do with Kristen, what I would do about catching the ones responsible for her mother's death, about Martin and his role in all this. I wanted to tell him, the entire story including gruesome details, but feared losing some of his respect that until now I had earned by just being me.

Herman Aguilar, who shook my hand and told me his name before he walked away, was broad shouldered, tall and impressive in his suit. But was in fact a man in turmoil, plagued by guilt about his daughter, his grandson. The nineties was a decade in which many parents lost their children in the fervor of reaching *la yuma* on anything that floated. There was a collective sadness amongst the Cuban people for those who never made it and the relatives they left behind. And almost everyone knew someone that knew someone that had lost someone. Herman and I hadn't just heard of someone who drowned or vanished, we had lost part of our lives to the ocean, to the vast Atlantic that meant freedom or death for the Cubans who defied it.

The next days flew by. Martin, Helen and I saw six locales for the new restaurant. None pleased Helen completely. Martin fell in love with the second locale down by the hospital. I didn't care. I liked all of them though I couldn't see how they would make one of these spaces into a fancy restaurant. I just couldn't see it. Most of these places needed the walls torn down and rebuilt. They were in such decrepit stages that Helen assured us they would not pass local inspections. Martin wasn't listening. He liked the place by the hospital and kept saying that's where he wanted the restaurant to be. They switched back and forth from English to Spanish for my benefit, when I coughed or signaled somehow I didn't understand, but then they'd go back to English until I'd signal again.

I didn't see much of Martin aside from the business outings we all did together. He didn't visit my room, didn't ask for sex, didn't even try to kiss me. It was the strangest thing for him to treat me like his girlfriend during the day, and then not even kiss me good bye when he left me, which was often right before dinner. The one time we had had dinner was with Helen present. Other than that, lunch, business talks and drives around the city were the only times I got to spend with him.

During my three days of crash intensive business training, I learned that Martin wasn't as sweet and nice as the night I'd met him, and that his interest in me was obviously not sexual. I learned that Helen wasn't as tough with Martin as she was with other people, and that their affinity to each other had more to do with how they benefited one another than actual attraction. There was no sexual tension between them, whereas I had begun to question if he wasn't having sex with me because he was having it with her, it was clear now that that wasn't happening. Martin wasn't sleeping with me not because of Helen, but because he didn't want to. And I didn't know why. I couldn't figure out what I had done wrong for him not to be interested in me anymore.

On the third morning of Martin's return to the island, I decided to ask him. I knocked on his door early, before the hustle and bustle of the hotel started. He answered as if he'd been standing right behind the door.

"This better be good at seven a.m.," he said.

"Can I come in?"

"Sure," he said sweeping the entrance way with his forearm. "Are you okay?"

"I'm fine," I said walking into the room. It looked as if no one had been in that room; the bed was made; nothing was out of place; the only things were the personal belongings on the night table.

"I want to ask you the same thing." His brow furrowed, and although he tried to pretend he didn't know what I was talking about, I knew he knew.

"Have I done something wrong?" I asked sitting on the corner of the bed. He turned his back to me, walked to a door I assumed was the bathroom and closed it.

"Milena, I didn't want to make you feel like you had to continue to be that young desperate girl I met a couple of weeks ago."

"But I'm not that girl any more, and you..."

"I just wanted it to come naturally from you, not because you owe me or I pay you."

"I understand, but then why are you doing all this for me?"

"Because I like you. Is that not good enough?"

"No one does anything just because they like me; they usually want more."

"Who is they? The people you've been dealing with? I hope I'm not included in that group."

"You're not, what I mean is..."

"Is that no one lately has done anything for you without expecting something back. Including me two weeks ago, right?"

I nodded. Didn't really know what to say to that.

"You know something Milena, the night you met me; I was sad; I was lonely; I was praying for something to make me want to get up in the morning. Then I find you walking the malecon."

Not sure of where he was going with this, I shifted my position on the bed, up on my left elbow, now paying close attention. If this was the moment of truth for him, it was going to be for me as well.

"I liked you immediately. I admired your tenacity at finding a client that night. I had seen you walk up and down the malecon a couple of times, and you wouldn't get on the street like the other girls. "

"I was scared; it was the first time I had worked alone."

"I could tell."

"Martin," I said sitting up, "I have to tell you something." He took a chair from the wooden set that had nothing on the table but two glasses upside down and straddled it.

"Let me just finish. I decided to try and help you that night. And when you didn't come back the next day, I knew something was wrong. So I asked Helen to find you. Unfortunately, I had to leave the island for business. But she found you, and now you are here, and you don't have to sleep with me to pay me for anything."

"Martin, I'm not nineteen. I'll be seventeen next month."

"I know," he said, standing up and walking towards the window. He stood there while I continued to blab about how sorry I was that I had lied to him without it registering that he already knew. He lit a cigarette by the window.

"You knew?"

"I don't really care that you lied to me, I know why you did it, but now I do care that you are actually so young."

"Is that why you don't come by my room?"

"Yes. I know you did what you thought you had to do with me for money. But you no longer have to do that."

"What if I want to?"

"I don't think you do. You think you do because it is the way you'll show me your gratitude. But what I want from you is to run this restaurant with Helen, and

    when you turn eighteen, you can make a decision whether you want to be with me or not."

"That's in a year."

"That's the right thing to do, Milena. You're still a girl in the eyes of the law."

"What happens if you've found someone in a year and you don't want me?"

"I haven't found anyone in ten so I doubt that's

going to happen. I plan to work hard for the next two or three years so I can retire. If you think then, you're still interested in this old man, then we can make further plans."

"I don't want to live in Cuba for the rest of my life, Martin, and to have you come to the island for a few days every so often and then you leave again; that is just like what I was last week. I want to get out of this country."

"I can't do anything until you turn eighteen, unless your legal guardian gives permission for me to marry you."

"I don't have a legal guardian."

"Your aunt is the only relative you have?"

I nodded.

"She's your guardian then," he said.

I thought about going back to my aunt's house, explaining to her what and where I had been for the past weeks, and then popping the question of the marriage certificate. But I was getting ahead of myself.

"You're saying you would marry me to get me out of here but you won't have sex with me?"

"I'm saying I don't want you to have sex with me because you think you have to pay me for something."

"But would you marry me?"

"Shouldn't I be the one to ask that?"

We both smiled. I thought my mother might have liked Martin for me, if he was younger. The age difference would have probably made her nervous reminding her of her own story with an older man who was married. But the fact that he was willing to marry me to get me out would have been enough for her. No one had ever asked her to get married. She used to tell me that she didn't want anyone, that no man was going to come between her and her daughter. But I knew she was lonely. After my father, she refused to date, and concentrated on her dancing, finding a way out and me.

"Are you asking now?"

He hesitated. Stood and removed the chair from between his legs, killed the cigarette in an ashtray by the window and sat next to me.

"Let me think about it, Milena. It isn't as easy as you think."

"A couple of my mom's friends from the dance company did it. One lives in Italy now and the other in Miami."

"Yes, but I bet they weren't in the same situation you are."

The two women my mother had known were dancers, and you had to be over eighteen to be able to dance in Tropicana.

"I don't know how to go back to my tia's house to ask for something like that."

"You don't have to."

"They're going to kill me if I stay in La Habana, Martin."

"No one's going to kill anybody."

"Then I'll end up in jail for something I didn't do."

"That's been taken care of. How do you think you are here?"

"How did Helen get me out if she is not my legal guardian?

"She paid people," Martin answered.

Couldn't she pay someone to become my legal guardian should have been my next question, but I didn't want to press the subject with Martin. It was becoming very clear that he didn't like to do things in a rush. He liked to make his own decisions, at his own pace, and didn't respond well to pressure. Helen on the other hand, moved like leech on skin when pushed.

CHAPTER EIGHT

I t was early morning. Today, Martin had to decide which locale would be better for the restaurant. Helen and I were sitting at the hotel's bar drinking coffee and waiting for him. It had now been seven days since she had taken me out of jail. I asked how she had done it, and if she could do the same to get me and Kristen out of the country now that Herman had found out she was still in the hospital.

"I don't know, but I'll see what I can do," was her response.

"What about him marrying me and taking me to Canada?"

"Look, Milena, you're asking me to do something that is not easy even when both parties are of legal age. Did he agree to the marriage?"

"He didn't disagree," I said.

"He didn't say have Helen take care of it, did he?"

I said no with my head. "You two are willing to help me as long as the benefits are tangible for both of you, isn't it?"

"That's unfair but if you want to believe it, believe it, because Martin is all about business first, second and third, then comes everything else."

"And you?"

"I'm the same." Suddenly, Martin stood there staring at us. I hadn't noticed and apparently neither had Helen. She took his elbow and walked out with him.

Ten minutes later they reappeared. Martin walked straight up to me. He said, "I told you I had to think about it."

"I need to know now."

"Why?"

"Because I found out my friend's baby is still in the hospital and I need to help her."

Martin looked at Helen. She shrugged. He looked back at me.

"You found? What do you mean? You haven't left the hotel alone, have you?"

"A friend found her for me."

"And now what are you planning to do?" Helen jumped in.

"I have no idea," I said.

Helen's electronic book vibrated on the bar. She looked at Martin.

"We gotta go, they're waiting for us," she told him.

I didn't feel like going anywhere, so I went back up to my room to think, to plan or to cry, not sure in what order. Herman was waiting for me to decide what to do with Kristen. Even if he was able to take her from the hospital, he couldn't bring her to the hotel.

With some cash Martin had left for me at the front desk, I took a cab to the motel where Margot had helped me. I knew I was risking finding the cops and/or Camacho, but I didn't have many options as far as what to do with Kristen. I told the driver to wait, gave him a ten dollar bill. At the front desk, a young man of about twenty asked me if I needed a room.

"No," I said, "I'm looking for Margot."

"She'll be here after two p.m.," he said.

An old clock on the wall said it was ten in the morning. I would come back then, I told the kid. The cab had taken off with my ten dollars. I should've known in a city like La Habana that you can't trust someone to provide a service when you've paid in advance. I walked the half mile back to the hotel.

On the way there, I could see the young girls ready to make their money for the day. I thought back a week, when I was here, looking for the same, looking for a way out. I thanked Yemaya for putting Helen and Martin in my path, and my mother, whom I had no doubt used her influence in heaven to push for the saint's help.

The city was still waking up. People walked out of their apartment buildings with sleepy eyes; a lady, still in her nightgown, yawned as her dog used the tire of a parked car to relieve himself. My mother and I always woke up early. It was a long habit of hers to wake up and exercise since her job required her muscles to be toned. On the weekends, after our café con leches (with whatever kind of milk was available) and whatever pieces of stale bread we could find, we would run along the bay in Regla. Even though she was one of the oldest dancers in Tropicana, she had the best pair of legs in La Habana. And running kept them tight. Then, if we had eggs, she'd fry two, skin a banana and mix it all in a bowl of rice that I'd devour almost immediately. She never ate right after exercising; she'd wait an hour before having to put whatever was left over in the refrigerator in her mouth.

My mouth was getting dry with the heat. It was so humid that my clothes were soaked with sweat before I reached the corner of Belascoain and Carlos Tercero. I stopped at an open window where two men drank coffee from. Asked the woman for a glass of water. She gave me a bottle, charged me one peso for it. I only had dollars, I told her. She shrugged, told me to give her a dollar then. A dollar was a lot to spend on water I knew came from city pipes since the top of the bottle had already been broken and the bottle did not look unused. But I needed the water to keep walking until I could hail a cab. It wasn't smart for me to walk the streets near el malecon; Camacho could be lurking in any corner. My only relief was that at ten in the morning he would've still been sleeping.

On the next street, I turned left, and two blocks down I turned right. The inner streets were less conspicuous, there were fewer people on them. By the time I had made it near the hotel, it was eleven-thirty. I didn't want to go in and have to explain to Martin or Helen where I'd been so I kept walking, past the hotel, past the malecon toward the hospital where Kristen was.

At the entrance, I stopped to look at my surroundings. I didn't have a clear idea of what I was going to do but I was here now, and I wanted to see the baby, to make sure she was okay. So I went inside, took the slow riding elevator to the children's floor. Once on the floor, I stayed close to the wall, like a soldier entering a dangerous place, and looked at my feet while walking. As usual, there were very few employees around. The nurses must have all been taking a break because no one was at the station. Lucky me.

The large Spartan room where the newborns were kept was at the end of the hall. I looked around before entering. The four incubators were placed at the far end of the room, and in between there were at least twenty tiny cribs with babies in them. I looked into the incubators first, only two had babies in them, and by the names on the tags, I could tell both were boys, which meant Kirsten was one of the twenty in the tiny cribs. At the head of each crib, there was a handwritten sign with the baby's name, birth weight and date, and the doctor in charge. I must have looked at ten or so before I found her. On the tag it said Garcia, Kristen. Even though Kristen's skin was darker than her mother's, her hair was exactly the same color as Kassandra's.

She looked healthy, no tubes, sleeping calmly with a faint smile on her lips. She had gained weight, was longer than I remembered, and her skin was now smooth and hydrated, not wrinkled like the first days after she was born.

As I reached to touch her, she woke up, looked at me and gave me one of those involuntary smiles babies give, but people believe is a true smile of recognition. My heart jumped. I picked her up, smelled her fuzzy head, her neck, looked at her little fingers and toes. She didn't make a sound. Her big eyes opened widely just staring at my face. I pressed her gently to my chest, squeezed her. She didn't make a sound, just breathed in and out slowly, as if taking in all the emotion coming out of me. I couldn't stop crying now.

All of a sudden three nurses came into the room laughing and making jokes. I ducked behind one of the cribs, baby in hands, very still. The nurses walked toward the back where the incubators were without a glance at the cribs. On my knees now, I placed Kristen in her crib and crouched down. I could hear the voices of the nurses but could not make out what they were saying. The cribs were an inch above my head, they couldn't see me from back there. In froglike position, I took two steps toward the door, then without much hesitation I squatted two steps back, got on my knees again in front of the crib. I took Kristen and the sheet she had been wrapped in, and held her tight to my chest with one hand, used the other hand for balance on the floor. I squatted all the way to the door, reached up with my free hand to open the door, and on the other side of the door stood and walked down the hall toward the elevator.

My chest was going to implode. Kirsten stared at me intently. Sweat covered every part of my body. I could feel the thick drops running down my spine, the back of my legs, my neck. I walked rapidly, not bothering to look around me for I was certain I would get caught.

At the nurses' station, a young girl in pale scrubs

answered the phones. She smiled at me while she bit her nail and held the phone with the side of her face. I smiled back, nervously, knowing that she would ask where I was taking the baby. But she didn't. She continued her conversation calmly, still gnawing her nail. I pressed the elevator button continuously. When the door opened, I stepped into the elevator hearing the nurses screaming when they found the empty crib, and I could swear I heard them. But when I turned to face the closing doors, there was no one. Out the main door I walked with Kristen in my hands without a peep.

The Caribbean sun was ruthless on the streets of La Habana that day. The danger I had just gotten myself into started to sink in. If I got caught, Helen would not be able to get me out of this one. By now, it must have been about one in the afternoon. Not a single taxi passed me, although I didn't think they'd stop if there were any passing by. Baby in hand was a sign that I was a Cuban without dollars, and cab drivers only wanted to take tourists who could pay in dollars. After walking about four blocks, I saw a bus station.

I waited for the next bus to anywhere. I needed to get out of the area, quickly, before the missing baby at the hospital sent out a search party of pigs all over La Habana. The bus was crowded, but at least it was running. In the last few months the government had cut at least half the bus routes. There was a shortage of gas, so only the most popular routes were running. The one I got on was going straight towards an area of La Habana I wasn't familiar with. I pulled the cord to be let out next stop.

Once off the bus, I wasn't sure where I was. I couldn't go back to the hotel with Kristen. Margot wouldn't be in for another hour. Soon, I realized I was on the same street as the house in which Kassandra and Camacho had rented a room.

At the next corner, the same one Kassandra had stood in the day we waited for Camacho to leave, I looked up at the windows. The room they kept was on the bottom floor, like the cellars of the old houses in La Habana Vieja. There were stairs that led directly to the second floor, without having to go into the house. I wondered if those were the stairs to Lucia's room. Kassandra had briefly mentioned the old lady rented out the rooms in the house to different people since she lived alone and the house was so big. I knew it was crazy to go right into where Camacho might still be living. But I had no one else to ask for help, and Kassandra had said that Lucia was like the grandmother she never knew. She might help me and Kristen now that she couldn't help Kassandra anymore.

The door to the upstairs part was closed but unlocked. I ran up the steps to another door. I knocked and tried the lock, but this one was locked. I knocked again, and again, harder each time. Nothing. Lucia must not be home, I thought, and walked down the steps. Just then, the old lady appeared within the frame of the outside door.

"Who are you?" she asked defensively. Like in any big city with huge financial problems, the older and the weak are prime targets for thieves. In La Habana of my mother's mother, whom I never met because she died before I was born, old people were revered, respected and for them to be a target for crime was unheard of. But times were different now.

"I'm Kassandra's friend; this is her baby, and I need your help," I said almost in tears.

"I haven't seen her in weeks." She asked going up the stairs toward me.

"She's dead," I said, squeezing Kristen tighter. The old woman stopped cold in the middle of the stairs.

"What happened?"

"She jumped out of a window."

"Ay dios mio," she cried, her body falling to the step above the one she was on.

I held Kristen with my left arm, and with my right reached for the old woman. But she had managed to stay seated on the step, her head in her hands. I sat next to her, switched Kristen to my right, put my left arm over Lucia's shoulders and cried, too.

"What are you going to do with her?" She asked between sobs as she reached for the baby.

"I don't know.

"Does Camacho know?"

I said no with my head. "Does he still live here?"

"No, I threw him out for not paying rent."

"I took her from the hospital. They'll soon be looking for us."

"Did anyone see you?"

"One of the nurses saw me walking out with the baby, but she was on the phone and didn't say anything to me."

Lucia adjusted Kristen in her bosom, ran her index

on the baby's cheek. "She looks just like her mother," she said.

"I know what Kassandra wanted for her daughter, and I feel responsible for her."

"Why?" she asked, now looking at me.

"I think if I would've stayed with her she wouldn't have done what she did."

"Let's go inside," she said handing me the baby who had started complaining meekly. "She has to be hungry. I have a can of evaporated milk I was saving for Kassandra."

I helped her up, even though she must have been close to ninety, her body was still jaunty, and she didn't need much help. Inside the top floor of the house, the conditions were not any different than any of the homes in La Habana. Everything was clean but old and falling to pieces.

"This is how I must live," she said referring to the condition of her home, "even though my husband was the owner of most of the property on this block before the Revolution."

There were two walls that had been built for the privacy of the renters that had reduced her living space to a large room with a makeshift kitchen, a bed and a t.v. stand that carried a set from the sixties. I didn't see any signs of a bathroom, and I needed one badly.

"You have to take the stairs to the bottom part," she said putting a small pot on one of the two portable gas burners that sat next to the sink. "The bathroom up here is clogged."

There was a small refrigerator and an old wooden table that housed a bottle of oil, a frying pan and two more pots. Everything was exposed as there were no cabinets, and the only window above the lone standing sink brought in dim lighting since few rays could escape the shadow of the building across the street.

"Those are Kassandra's things," Lucia said pointing with her chin to a bag that sat patiently in a dark corner. "I always thought she would come back to see me. I was the only person she really cared for after her mother left for Europe."

I was desperate for a bathroom, but didn't want to lose the story. Kassandra had mentioned what her mother did, and that she had left, but she never mentioned where to. And I assumed it had been to Miami, where all the balseros went.

"Europe? She didn't go to Miami?"

"Naw, she met a much older man who fell in love with her and took her to his country. Belgium, I think it was."

"Why didn't she take Kassandra?"

"Ay mija, who knows? Kassandra was already eighteen and doing her own thing with Camacho. I don't know why a mother would leave her daughter with those kinds of people but..."

"Did Kassandra ever say she wanted to go with her?"

"She regretted not leaving with her mother when she had the chance to. But she was in love with that piece of shit, and thought he loved her as well."

I excused myself for the bathroom. I couldn't hold

it any longer. Going downstairs brought vivid memories of Kassandra, of the day I met her, the day we came here, showered, and she looked desperately for the money she put in her boots. The day she died, her body strewn on the pavement encircled by thickening blood.

The small room was now empty, the bathroom clean, nothing thrown on the floor. I started to pee soon realizing there was no toilet paper. There was never any toilet paper in Cuba. It was a commodity, like meat and milk when it came, and the monthly six rolls the government gave you soon went.

So I sat there, air drying, thinking. Thinking about Kassandra's mother, if I could find her she would help her granddaughter. If not, then I'd have to ask Helen to help me with Kristen. Ultimately, Helen would need Martin's approval to do anything, the question was if Martin would be willing to help with so delicate a subject.

"I have an extranjero who might help but if not, can you?" I asked her as I walked back into the upstairs room. She was feeding Kristen with a dropper.

"I can't do much. I don't have dollars and you see how I live. But I'll help in whatever I can."

"Do you know anything about Kassandra's mother"?

"Nothing other than what I've told you."

"Are you sure Camacho won't come back?"

"If he does, he can't get in downstairs or up here. The family who rents the room from me next door, they know who he is. They won't even look at him. Everyone around here knows what kind of son-of-a bitch he is."

I loved the fact that Lucia cursed. Her lips, pursed and wrinkled, pronounced the bad words fully as if tasting a succulent steak.

"I need you to stay with the baby. I can't take her anywhere because the cops are going to be looking for me."

"They'll find her here. This is the first place they're going to come looking for him," she said.

"Won't they first go to his house in La Habana Vieja?"

"I don't know where they'll go first, but they're going to come here for sure."

She was right, of course. The first suspect would be the alleged father, but then the young nurse would confess to seeing me walk out with the baby and they'd know immediately who I was. I should've thought things through and gone back in disguise, or have Herman take her as I had originally thought. But it was done now. Only place to go was forward.

"I can't be seen running around Centro Habana with a baby. Can you take her to a friend's house while I go get help?"

"I can go down the street to have a cafe with my friend, but not for too long. And whose baby am I going to say this is? People around here know I don't have any grandchildren."

"Tell them you're babysitting."

"Babysitting? Everybody knows everybody around here. No one's had a baby."

"I don't know; tell them it's your nephew's or

something."

"How do I know you're not going to just take off and leave me here with this baby?"

"I promise I'll come for her."

She put the tip of the dropper into the pot, squeezed the black rubber top so the milk could be sucked up by the glass, and put it to Kirsten's tiny lips.

"I loved Kassandra, and I'll help you, but I can't be responsible for this baby at my age."

"I just need you to watch her for an hour or so while I go get help. I think I know someone who will help me with her."

Lucia nodded; the bun in the back of her head wobbled. She gave me the baby, and the dropper, said she'd be right back. As she walked to the corner where the bag of Kassandra's stuff was resting, she let go of the bun completely, rearranged it, and pinned it to her head again. She had long strands of completely white hair, and now that I looked at her from a distance, I could tell even at her golden age that she had been a very beautiful woman.

She bent down in front of the bag and opened it. Several things were bursting out of the bag, one of them was a small make-up bag that Lucia grabbed and brought to me. She took the baby and the dropper back.

"Open it," she said. I did. A wad of dollar bills was folded together. "I kept all the loose change and dollars that fell out of that asshole's pocket for a year, and saved it for her. I hoped when she had the baby she'd decide to leave him and she was going to need that money."

I counted the bills. Five twenties, three tens, and twenty one dollar bills.

"She was a good girl; it's too bad she didn't use her head right."

"She really didn't have many options," I said, more to convince myself of my lack of options than to convince her.

She nodded, continued to feed the baby. I put the money in my pocket; the rest of the dollars Martin had given me were in a small bag I carried off my shoulder.

"I won't leave her; you have my word," I said bending to kiss the baby's forehead. I stared at her big green eyes while she sucked on the tip of the dropper.

"If you do, I'm going to have to give her to the authorities," she said.

It was now close to three p.m. Margot would be at work and I could get a room to keep Kristen in with Lucia while I went to the hotel to talk to Helen. Hopefully she and Martin had returned from signing the contract for the restaurant, and I could ask her to meet me downstairs.

I ran to the bus stop on the opposite side of the street, waited for about five minutes when a taxi passed me. I stood in the middle of the street to stop it. It had no choice but to stop and the man behind the wheel cursed at me. I showed him a five dollar bill; he signaled for me to jump in.

Margot was behind the counter doing paperwork when I walked into the small lobby. She wasn't too happy to see me.

"I told you not to come back here," she said going back to her paperwork.

"I need your help again, please."

"I can't help you anymore; I can't lose my job and you got people looking for you all over. You're going to get me in trouble."

"Please," I said, hands in prayer under my chin. "I need to talk to you."

She looked both ways as if crossing a busy street, and signaled for me to go to the back where the barbacoa was.

"What is it?"

"I need someone to watch a baby for me; I have dollars to pay with."

"A baby? Your baby?"

"No, my friend's."

"Where's your friend?"

"Dead."

"I don't want anything to do with it." She said as she started to walk away. I grabbed her elbow.

"Por favor, Margot, I have no one else. I can pay one hundred dollars for someone to watch this baby."

I don't know if it was the mention of the hundred dollars, but she hesitated, rescued her elbow from my grip, and told me to wait. At the front desk, a jinetera and her client wanted a room.

When they left, Margot poked her head in, said to stay put, she was going next door to talk to her sister. I wiped my sweaty palms on my thighs thinking that if anyone walked in while she was gone, I'd have to come outside before they walked in straight to the back looking for the attendant.

I closed my eyes and prayed to all the orishas to keep Kristen safe; to Yemaya specifically to help me, and to Chango who had been Kassandra's saint. Even though I'd never been too religious, I knew more about Santeria from hearing about it than I did about Catholicism. I figured if I prayed to the orishas, perhaps they would strike down upon Padrino and Camacho who pretended to be firm believers, and they would help Kristen in order to honor her mother who truly believed in them.

When I opened my eyes, Margot and another woman stood in front of me; both with identical grins on their faces.

"Why is she praying, Margot?" the woman who looked exactly like Margot but with badly bleached blonde hair asked.

"This is my twin sister," Margot said. "She'll watch the baby in her house next door. You have to pay in advance for the hours you'll be gone, and if you're not back by then, we take the baby to the cops."

The sister nodded and Margot crossed her arms on her chest waiting for my response. I nodded as well, reached into my pocket and took out the cash Lucia had given me. In the bag were the two hundred dollars Martin had given me, but I only handed Margot the wad of money in my hands. I'd need some cash to get around.

"Not sure how much is there," I said.

The blonde counted. "A hundred dollars," she said.

I hadn't spent the fifty-one dollars on the way here

so I was sure she lied, but I didn't care. I needed her help.

"Okay," I said. "So you'll watch her for a couple of hours?"

"Yea, but I don't have diapers or milk. You have to get that for her."

"I'll be back with everything she needs. But I need you to go get her at this address. Its close by."

"That wasn't what you told me," the bleached blonde said to her sister.

"How close?" Margot asked me. I gave them the address. The blonde agreed for an additional fifty dollars when I came back with the supplies.

I stepped out into the humid afternoon; it was now close to four p.m.. If I didn't hurry back, Martin would send Helen to my room and they'd know I'd stepped out alone; something I wasn't supposed to do until I went in front of a judge to explain what I was doing on the ledge of the window my friend had jumped out of.

No taxis, no buses, only people riding bikes and the few twenty-year old cars that rode on the boulevard. There were a few of the newer cars that only tourists could rent, one tour guide bus filled with Europeans on their way to the outskirts of the city, and the rest were people on foot. I walked briskly up the street toward the hotel contemplating taking the inner streets, away from the malecon and the busy boulevard, but it would take me longer to get to the hotel.

The lobby was busy, as usual, with lots of tourists and employees of the hotel. No one seemed concerned with me anymore so I went straight to the elevator and up to my room. I dialed Helen's room. No answer. Martin's room; no answer either. I went down

The bartender approached us, asked if I wanted a Coca-Cola. I nodded.

"I saw you walk in from the street. Where were you?" Helen asked. She took a long sip of her drink and a long drag of her cigarette. I took a deep breath, waited for the bartender to serve the drink, took a long swag of it, and started.

"I had to take care of something."

"You know you can't be out there doing what you were doing before?"

"I went to the hospital to see my friend's baby."

"What is it with you and this baby?"

"I need to save her."

"You need to save yourself first if you want to save anyone. You're not completely off the hook with the law, you know?"

"Martin said that had been taken care of."

"I bailed you out, but you still have to go in front of a judge and tell your story. It's not clear your friend committed suicide."

"She jumped out of her bedroom window!"

"Her family is saying you pushed her."

"Of course they're blaming me, they're not even her real family. What's not clear is what they were trying to put into her mouth."

"I told you I'm not interested in stories. Tell yours to the judge. Meanwhile, stay out of trouble, and the only way for you to do that is to stay in your room."

I sipped my Coca-Cola, she sipped her drink, smoked, looked around. Not sure how I would tell her what I had just done, I asked the bartender to pour some rum in my drink. He looked at Helen for approval. She shrugged.

"I stole the baby from the hospital," I said with the straw still in my mouth looking at the swirling liquid in the cup.

"You did what?"

"I went to see her and just walked out with her."

"Are you out of your fucking mind? Being accused of something is one thing, but kidnapping a baby in broad daylight from a hospital? Forget it! You're going to jail!"

"I don't want to go to jail, Helen."

"Then why the fuck do you keep breaking the law?"

I felt like a kid who has just been caught doing something terribly wrong.

"I don't know but it's done now. And I need your help."

"Does Martin know?"

"No."

"You better tell him because I don't think I can help you with this one."

"Helen please, you know a lot of people in this island. You know people in the hospital that can help."

"How's that?"

"I don't know how, not sure even of my next step, but..."

"But you expect me to figure it out for you?"

"I'm not expecting anything. I'm hoping."

"Well keep hoping, little girl, because I'm not getting my hands dirty with this one. This is serious and I don't need to get involved."

"If you don't help, she'll become a jinetera by the time she's eleven."

"How's that my problem?"

"It's my problem. I'm asking you to help me. I know you care about me."

She swallowed what was left in her glass, signaled for the bartender to serve another one and killed the cigarette on a nearby ashtray.

"I think you're confused about caring and doing one's job. Martin asked me to find you. When I did, you were in jail for attempted murder, he asked me to take you out, I did. Now you think I care about you. I care about my job, which is the only thing I have."

She drank half her new drink in two big gulps. It seemed she was angry but her eyes looked down at the drink as if in it were long lost stories of her past. And it was sadness, not anger, her spirit declared.

"Why is it the only thing you have? Where's your family?" I sipped my rum and Coca-Cola, slowly, because in Cuba when you ate or had anything American you savored it, you saved it, as it may be a long while before you'd get your hands on it again.

"Don't have any."

"No parents, no relatives, nothing?"

"My mother died when I was your age, never knew who my father was."

"Like me," I said, watching her take another huge swallow of her drink.

"But I never stole a baby from a hospital." Another gulp and her glass empty, she signaled again for the bartender.

"You don't have any kids?"

"No."

"No husband?"

"I'm divorced. What are you the defense committee of the Revolution to be asking all these questions?"

I smiled. On each block in La Habana, the government had designated a house to be the enforcer of the Revolution. Tourists didn't know these details. But Helen was not a tourist.

"Why did you get divorced?"

"I left him for a co-worker, then she left me for her boss."

"She?" I asked with a huge smile. Sip, sip, she was letting me in.

"Yes, I was married to a man, but I'm a lesbian."

"And she? Is she still a lesbian?"

"No, her boss is a man. They're married now."

"And you've never found anyone else?"

She said no with her head, gulped her drink and took out a cigarette from her purse. "I like being alone," she slurred. I'd never heard her voice drunk.

"I don't," I said. "I miss my mother."

"You'll get used to it."

"You don't miss yours?"

"I'm used to being without her. I've had to do without her for years now."

I was amazed at the amount of alcohol she could

hold down. I was still on my first and she was already on her third drink, since I'd been sitting there anyway. Her face was starting to show clear signs of drunkenness; her hair, disheveled and flowing freely all over her face. She spread her fingers through it as if by doing so she would regain some lucidity.

A long silence followed. She smoked, drank, smoked, drank. Not a word from either of us. I was finished with my drink and felt a little tingling in my stomach. I now had less than three hours to go back to Margot to get Kristen, and still I had no idea what to do.

The bald headed, hateful little man who was the manager appeared at the door of the bar and walked directly toward us.

"She has to go," pointing at me. "I can't keep covering up for her."

"What?" Helen said, the vowels dancing a rough dance with her tongue.

"You heard me. The big boss is coming in tomorrow morning, and you know Cubans are not allowed in the hotels. I know Mr. Brodstein has been more than generous with me and my staff, but now I can't do anything anymore."

He didn't look my way but stared at Helen, who in her stupor was not in the best of moods.

"What if she stays with me in my room?" Helen asked.

"Can't do it," he said, "can't have any Cubans on the property. You guys know this is the law."

"A fucked-up law!" Helen yelled. Everyone at the

bar looked our way. The bald headed guy shrunk into his suit, his cheeks turning the hue of Helen's red blouse.

"Ms. Davenport, please don't yell at me. There's nothing I can do. I wish I could, but you know I've been more than accommodating to you and Mr. Brodstein."

It struck me then how pleasant and polite this man was with Helen. He had never even said hello to me, although he'd seen me plenty of times. But he spoke to Helen as if she were royalty.

"Stupid fucking law. I've never been in a country where its own citizens can't be in the hotels. How do you people put up with that?" She exhaled the smoke into the manager's face. As he coughed, she laughed. "What do you suppose I do with this one?" she said loudly, now pointing an index at me.

"I have a friend who can rent you a house for a week or two."

She inhaled again, swallowed the rest of her drink, and stood. She was visibly drunk, and the manager reached out a hand to help her. She slapped it out of her way.

"Don't need your fucking help, I'm fine," the last two words dragging. "tell me about a house?"

He explained to us that the houses in Centro Habana could be rented for a portion of what the hotel rooms cost, and we could do whatever we wanted in there; no restrictions.

"How much for a month?"

"I don't know, you gotta talk to my friend about that."

I was a fly on the wall, listening, already plotting in my head how to bring Kristen to the rented house. Thank you, Yemaya.

"Where is he? Bring him to me." She ordered him like one would a slave.

He didn't say anything but turned on his heel and walked out.

"I guess you're getting what you want," Helen said, an obvious struggle to get her tongue to listen to her brain. She took a step forward and bumped her hips into the stool. I stood to help her, took her arm and guided her outside. Some people looked at us though most just went about their business.

With Helen's heavy arm around my shoulders, we reached the elevator. She said she wanted to go to her room to shower and sober up, and that I should go to mine to pack my things. I agreed.

I stuck my prized possessions--four outfits and two pairs of shoes--into a duffel bag Helen had given me. The toothbrush, which had been brought to my room along with some toothpaste and soap, I stuck in the small bag with the money from Martin. In less than ten minutes, I was out the door in the direction of Helen's room.

She opened the door wearing nothing but her towel, her hair tied up in a bun on top of her head, her make up running down her cheeks, and still trying to shake off the effects of about three drinks in less than forty-five minutes. She invited me in, said she'd be just a minute to get dressed. I took two steps in, closed the door but stayed near it. She released the bun to show long strands of orangy-red hair, different than Kassandra's red, yet so strikingly similar. Her room was the same as mine, not as fancy as Martin's. She went into the bathroom and two minutes later came out wearing the same clothes.

"Don't have anything clean," she declared.

I didn't care what she wore. I was used to wearing the same clothes for days on end when there was no detergent to wash them with. I shrugged. She took the mass of red hair, pulled it back into a pony tail and tied it.

"Let's go," she said, already walking toward the door.

"Ah, did you look at your face?"

"What's wrong with my face?" she walked in the direction of the bathroom.

"Aw, shit. Thanks for telling me," she said, and washed her face.

She came out of the bathroom drying her face. "You don't seem too upset about having to leave."

"I'm not actually. I'm going to..."

"No, no, no, don't tell me. Don't wanna know!"

She was going to help me, but she didn't want to acknowledge it. That's fine with me, I thought.

"I was just going to say that I'm going to miss this place with the luxuries and all..." a bubbling sarcasm in my words.

She threw the hand towel on the floor without taking her eyes off me.

"You're too much like me," she said reaching for the doorknob and opening the door.

It was close to six p.m. now, and I had only a couple of hours before I had to get Kristen. I was hoping the matter of renting the house could happen quickly.

The manager approached us as soon as we were out of the elevator. Herman was approaching us from the other direction. Helen walked toward the fancy sofas and took a seat. I did the same.

"Ms. Davenport, Ms. Campos, this way, please," Herman said motioning with his arm for us to follow him toward the back of the lobby.

"Why that way? The main door's this way," Helen said without moving an inch.

"It's safer this way," answered Herman. "Trust me."

I stood to follow him. I trusted him. Because of him I had found Kristen. Helen hesitated a second, but then decided to follow us outside by the pool exit. All this time no one had thought about Martin who was by the outside bar having a beer and reading a newspaper I could make out to be American, because of its large pages.

Helen immediately walked over to him, took a chair and started to talk. I waited with Herman by my side, the manager excused himself and went back in.

"Let's go wait in the car," Herman said.

Once in it, I updated him on what had happened with Kristen.

"That's very gutsy, Milena. But now what? What are you going to do with her? You can't keep her, you know that."

"I can't let that devil get his hands on her."

"She's not yours, Milena; she belongs to her family."

"She has no family. Her mother is dead and the only people that want her will turn her into a jinetera by the age of ten."

His eyes focused on mine as if trying to decipher where the determination to save this baby had come from.

"I know it's crazy, Herman, but please just help me."

"I can't do much; the house you're going to be staying in is very close to here, and you're still in Camacho's range. You have to leave La Habana if you really don't want to be found."

"I know, I'll figure it out," I said unsure whether I actually could.

After a long silence, Herman finally said, "My wife has a house in Matanzas. It's being rented now, but I can arrange to have it empty by the end of next month."

Matanzas was the province next to La Habana; it had the second biggest city in Cuba, the most beautiful of all the beaches on the island called Varadero, and aside from La Habana's bursting population of tourists, I had heard Matanzas was pretty much the same.

"But Matanzas? It's far, no? I've never been to the city, only to Varadero."

"It's three hours by train, one and a half by car."

"Three hours?"

"She could rent you a car," he said meaning Helen.

"She doesn't want to help me with anything that has to do with Kristen."

"She's getting you this house!"

"Only because I can't stay at the hotel anymore. Right now, she's getting his approval. She doesn't make a move without it."

"I know. Can you ask him?"

"He doesn't want to get involved in anything illegal."

Herman shrugged his shoulders. "He's not the most law abiding extranjero. Everybody knows the Cuban government looks the other way because of all the dollars tourists bring in. But many of them are still paying for sex with underage girls. And that's illegal."

"I'm not sleeping with him." I announced looking toward the hotel. "He doesn't want to, not sure why."

"Maybe he's developed a conscience over the last week he's been here."

"I lied to him; he thought I was nineteen when I met him."

"It still doesn't make it right, Milena. These men come to our country with a few dollars and they pervert our girls. They dangle a nice meal, a few pairs of underwear and shoes, maybe some jeans or a nice dress, and they've got a young body to play with in exchange."

"But he's not like that. I'm telling you he doesn't want to have sex with me, not until I turn eighteen next year."

"I guess your consolation could be to think of how

many girls out there would give anything to be in your shoes."

"I don't think I'm so lucky; I must have pissed off the orishas because look at all the trouble I'm in."

"I don't believe in Santeria, but you have to trust God; he is only testing you."

"How many more tests, Herman? I lost my mother. In less than two weeks I've stolen money from men, I've had sex with men for money, I think I'm failing all the tests!"

"It will make you into a better person."

"Not if I end up in jail," I said leaning back into the seat. In the distance, I could see Helen walking toward the car.

"You won't," Herman said, opening the door and stepping out to meet Helen.

"Let's go," she said, and got inside. She didn't look at me but fiddled with her little book.

From the rearview mirror, Herman looked at me, then at Helen, then back to me. I could tell he was nervous because beads of sweat ran down his forehead.

"You know, Helen," he started, "I have a house in Matanzas, near Varadero, that you can rent very cheap."

"In Matanzas?"

"Have you ever been to Varadero?"

"Once. I hate the beach."

He looked at me through the mirror again. Helen kept focused on her book, didn't even glance up at me or him.

"I love the beach," I said, "especially Varadero. It's so beautiful."

"I don't like getting full of sand, so I never go," she said, eyes still on book.

"Maybe Martin wants to go? Does he like the beach?" Herman said.

"Have you looked at his skin?" she answered.

Martin's skin was past the simple sunburn of a day; it was cooked like a Cuban steak, well done and stiff. Herman smiled, a hint of victory in his eyes.

"I think he'll want to go," he said.

"Yes, he told me he needs a break," I said lying.

"A break? Are you sure he told you he needs a break? He hasn't told me anything."

"I ah...well he didn't really...he said that...."

"If he likes the beach, Varadero is the place to go," Herman said.

Helen looked up at me from her little book, then at Herman. "All right, what's going on with you two? What are you plotting?"

I looked out the window at the people walking by. It was an August evening, around six, a humid, moldy smell rose from the pavement, all windows in the car were open, only the tourist cars had air conditioning. There was a brief dead silence.

"Did you guys sign the contract for the restaurant?" I asked.

"No, he wants me to find another place. Don't change the subject. What's going on? I'm not stupid, you know!"

"We know, Helen," I said, giving in to my secret

after a strained pause. "I need to leave La Habana."

"What do you mean, you need to leave? You can't leave."

"I have to. No one will look for me in Matanzas."

"Have you gone insane?" Helen continued.

"She has a point, Helen," Herman interjected again. "Who's going to look for her in Matanzas?"

"The law is going to look for her everywhere. She could be charged with murder."

"I think if they were going to charge her with murder, they would've done so already."

Score point for Herman! Helen was quiet, a rare thing for her to be in the middle of an argument. The light turned green, the car moved. I looked out the window worried that she might be right and they would come look for me even in Matanzas.

We stopped front of a house on stilts; these on 2x4 crutches. The neighborhood of El Vedado was famous for its beautiful turn of the century houses. Many were rented out to tourists for the week, two weeks or monthly. Cubans were well accustomed to living with immediate family members such as sisters and husbands, parents and even first cousins. In a three-bedroom house you could find twelve people, each bedroom with a barbacoa gave enough space for a family of four. Each family, living off the illegal income of the rented house, was able to buy food and basic necessities, albeit sacrificing the privacy of their homes. But it was better to give up your home to live with other people with a full stomach, than stay alone in your big house with nothing in the fridge.

Helen stepped out of the car slowly, still thinking I suppose, because she was way too quiet. She examined the house that, having been built some eighty years before, still retained its original structure.

"Who lives here?" she asked Herman.

"Nobody. The family left by El Mariel."

"No one has lived here in thirteen years?"

"Only tourists who rent it."

"Who rents it to the tourists?"

"The state," answered Herman.

"And who collects the rent for the state?"

"I do," he answered. "I've been doing it since the family left to Miami."

"And I suppose you decide how much is the rent?" Helen asked, her voice dripping with sarcasm.

"I can decide how much 'above' what the state wants."

"How much does the state want for it?"

"Two hundred dollars a week."

"How much do you charge the tourists?"

"Depends. I'm not making any money with you renting it, if that's what you want to know."

"Why not?"

"I want to help her," he said pointing to me.

"Good," she said walking towards the front door of the house, "because she needs all the help she can get."

He frowned, but I signaled quiet with my index. I didn't want to get Helen started on all the trouble I was in and how she and Martin had helped me. As a matter of fact, I thought it needless and repetitive for her to even mention it, but left it alone knowing that arguing with her would serve me nothing but a worse headache than I already had.

Herman's watch said six forty-five. In less than an hour, I'd have to bring Kristen back here. Herman opened the front door. A strong rotten odor confronted my nostrils; it reminded me of Padrino's house. Helen made a comment about it. Inside, the house was scarcely furnished with psychedelic pieces from the sixties and seventies. A yellow rustic couch accompanied by a red and an orange bean bag called my attention; I had never seen such modern furniture in any of the homes I'd ever visited. In my own house, my mother had kept the furnishings her mother had left her, and that she, my grandmother, had inherited from her own mother. So I grew up with furniture that was at least forty or fifty years old.

There were two red and black rectangular lamps on glass tables at each end of the couch. Only fancy places like hotels had glass tables. On the ceiling, the light bulbs were covered with glass globes, not naked like in most Habana apartments. The kitchen, spacious and fully equipped, included a microwave, a very rare commodity in Cuba.

"So two hundred for the week?" Helen asked Herman.

He nodded.

"I'm going to give you three to keep an eye on her and get some groceries."

"You don't have to give me anything to take care

of her. Just let her have a few dollars to buy some food with."

"Take the extra hundred for food then," she said taking the money out of her bag and handing it to him.

I would need to buy some powdered baby milk with that money, I thought. Helen walked around the house. I followed her to the two bedrooms directly in front of each other with a bathroom in the middle. The room with the big bed had very little furniture other than a mirror leaning against the wall facing the bed. The other had two small beds, and a nightstand between them. I heard Helen's corky laugh coming from the big bed, so I walked over to the door of the room.

"I bet the clients love this, huh Herman?" Helen said sprawling out her arms on the bed.

"They do," he said standing at the door to the room. "And they pay good money for it."

"Love what?" I asked.

"The mirror," Helen pointed at it with her high heeled foot.

I didn't care. All I could think of was getting back to Kristen, and bringing her here. El Vedado was out of the way, at least ten miles from el malecon; she'd be safe here.

"Herman, can you give us a minute?" Helen asked. He walked out of the room.

"You know, Martin's going to pass by to see the house."

"I have to bring her here."

"You shouldn't bring anyone here."

"They're going to call the cops if I don't go get her in less than an hour."

She paused to look at me. "Then I suggest you tell him."

"After. I don't have much time now."

She took two steps toward me, defensively but cautious. "I wouldn't tell him after the fact."

"I have to." I held her stare a while longer, then walked out of the room. Herman was waiting by the door.

"Ready?" He asked.

"Wait."

Helen walked out of the room, fixed her hair, and asked to go. There was such a decisive tone in everything she said that even if she asked for something nicely, it sounded like an order. Herman and I followed her orders. In the car, I realized she wasn't angry when she patted my thigh and said I was going to be okay, before turning her attention to her little book. No one spoke.

When Herman pulled over beside the hotel, Helen got out without a word. She closed the car door slowly, and walked into the hotel. Herman looked at me through the mirror and asked where to.

Margot was giving some change to a customer when I walked up to the front desk. I waited. As soon as the customer left, she said, "Thank god," and signaled for me to follow her outside. The apartment building next to the motel was in no better condition than the motel itself. Its flaky baby blue paint was in stark contrast to the crumbling orange of the motel's façade. Herman waited in the car.

"Did you get the extra cash for my sister?"

"Yes."

"Milk and diapers?"

"Didn't have a chance to get that."

"She's been crying a lot. We gave her some watered down condensed milk, and she was quiet for about an hour. She started again about ten minutes ago."

I just nodded, as if I knew what to do for a crying baby. I followed Margot into the building that housed three or four families in each apartment. Its halls littered with toys, cigarettes and bottles of booze were occupied by its tenants sitting on foldable chairs, leaning against their doors or on the handrails.

Margot went into one of the apartments on the first floor, told me to wait outside. I looked around to the center of the open patio where people stood around the domino tables where games were bet on. I leaned next to the door. I was nervous about Kristen. I had babysat before, but older kids, never a tiny baby like her. If I got caught, there was no question I'd be in jail for a long time, and Kristen would end up just like her mother.

Margot came out with a quiet, covered bundle in her arms. "My sister borrowed a cloth diaper from a neighbor, and she changed her. So she'll be good for a little bit. But you have to feed her soon."

"Okay," I said, extending my arms to receive the bundle. Kristen's eyes were halfway closed as she fought sleep. She was such a beautiful baby. As soon as

I put her close to my chest, her eyes finally closed and she slept peacefully. I, too, felt peaceful and purposeful that someone depended on me.

I followed Margot outside where Herman held one of the car's back-door open. I quickly got in and rolled the window down.

"Thank you," I said to Margot. "I don't know what I would've done without you."

"You're welcome." She said hanging her hands through the window. "Get out of the city if you can." She patted the inside of the door, said adios, and quickly made her way back into the motel.

Herman took off through the streets of La Habana while Kristen slept in my arms. I thought about Margot's advice to leave the city. To Miami, ideally, but that was expensive. Soon, we were in El Vedado, nearing the rented house.

"I know a bodega that accepts dollars; I can get the milk and diapers," Herman said turning onto the street the house was on.

"Thank you. I wouldn't know where to go."

"You should listen to what she told you and leave."

"To Matanzas?"

"To wherever. It'll be less than a week before they find you here."

"I don't have enough money to rent your house."

"Talk to Martin. Maybe he'll help."

"Maybe," I said. "What if he doesn't?"

"I can talk to my wife. It's her parents' house even though the government holds the deed."

"Does she know about me?"

"I told her how I met you."

"And she's okay with that?"

"You remind us of our daughter; we don't judge you."

"Is that the only reason you're helping me?"

"You need a bit of guidance at the moment."

"I think I need a lot of guidance, Herman. I don't know how I'm going to get out of this one."

"Ask Martin for help," he said pulling in front of the house.

I scurried out of the back seat with Kristen still asleep. Herman gave me the key to the front door, got back behind the wheel and pulled away. I watched the back of the car turn the corner, went into the house, put the baby on the big bed with all the pillows surrounding her in case she woke up, and stepped into the living room to see about the foul smell. It seemed to be coming from the small balcony at the end of the kitchen. I opened the door to find a rotting dove's corpse lying on the tile. The smell was more pungent outside. Doves were traditionally used in Santeria offerings to substitute for the chickens that people could eat. But this house had only been rented to tourists for the past thirteen years. Rituals and offerings were usually done for good, but the dark side of the religion could also be used to do wrong, and rotting animals were left to drive people out. Whatever ritual had been done to whoever inhabited the house before, I knew could not harm us. But I also knew that touching a rotting corpse of an animal that has been used in a ritual could bring about sickness and disease. So I closed the sliding glass door; the rotting bird would just have to wait.

In the other room, Kristen complained of hunger and wetness. I tried to rock her back and forth, but the peaceful look she had on her face when I walked out of the hospital with her, was now a desperate cry of discomfort. My nerves shot up at the sound of the intense cries. The tiny person in my arms, who would not stop screaming at the top of her lungs, was now turning a deep plum color. I walked around with her on my shoulder. I sat down and put her on my lap. I tried singing *las mañanitas*, to no avail. I put Kristen on the bed, a pillow on each side to prevent her from rolling, and to somewhat muffle the cries.

I unwrapped the thin hospital blanket. She wore just the cloth diaper with two big pins on each side, and a tiny white t-shirt that had been washed too many times. I felt the cloth soaked to the last thread. On the inside of the blanket, a pacifier hung by a small pin. I imagined it was Margot's sister who put it there; hospitals in Habana didn't have sheets, much less pacifiers. I unhooked it and put it to Kristen's mouth. She sucked on it ravenously, the screaming subsiding for the moment. I removed the pins on each side of her hips. The urine was beginning to seep through to the sheets on the bed. I took the corner of the top sheet, and easily pulled it apart. With it, I made a diaper under Kristen's hips, and pinned the corners. I threw the sodden diaper in the sink. The baby seemed more calm, her eyes opening and closing in a battle with sleep. I knew soon she'd start crying again, this time for milk. I lay next to her.

There was an invisible mallet pounding on the back of my head. Kristen had given up her fight with sleep. I imagined what my mother would have done in my situation. She most definitely would've taken Kristen away to a safe place. Not even the outskirts of the city were safe in my case. El campo was the only place the cops wouldn't find me; they'd just assume I took a raft to Miami, and either made it or drowned.

Even if Helen and Martin decided not to help me, I could move to Matanzas, work in the fields, save enough money to get on a boat to Miami, even if it took years.

I could say Kristen was mine and that I lost her birth certificate, this I didn't really think would work. But one could hope that in a small town, no one would suspect.

A loud knock. Herman had been lucky finding everything so quickly. I peeled myself from the bed carefully so as not to wake Kristen, and rushed to open the door.

"You didn't think I was going to wait until you invited me to come see this place, did you?" Martin said standing at the door.

"I ah...I just got here myself, I was going to tell you."

"I know you were. Can I come in?"

"Sure," I said, moving to the side and clearing the way for him.

"Helen said you had something to tell me."

"She did, huh?" I said, closing the door behind me.

"Sit down," I pointed to the yellow couch.

"Aren't you going to show me around first?"

"I want to talk to you first," I said, heading to the couch myself. Martin followed.

"I took my friend's baby from the hospital. She's in the bedroom." Martin showed no emotion for my confession; he just waited. "I don't know what I'm going to do yet, but I need your help."

He exhaled, a long held breath, it seemed, and nestled his forehead in his hands. "I can't help you, Milena. You have to understand."

"What do I have to understand?"

He looked up at me. "That the result of my life's work, most of my money, is here and I can't be involved in anything illegal."

"But I need your help."

"I've been helping, but this is where I draw the line."

"What about you and me?" I dared to ask.

"What about it, Milena? I told you you're just way too young."

"In a year I'll be eighteen. Is that old enough?"

"We'll see then. I'll be in La Habana."

"I won't," I said.

"It's just going to have to be destiny then."

Destiny? What did Destiny have to do with anything? "Martin, you really just don't feel anything for me?" I asked getting close to his face.

"Actually," he said, pulling away from me. "I find myself attracted to you. But you're just a girl. It is against the law."

"You don't always follow the law."

"I don't, especially in business. But this isn't business."

"You're more risky with your business than with your personal life? That doesn't make sense."

"I'm more cautious with my personal life, yes."

"How come?"

"That's just the way I am. I don't like to take chances when it comes to matters of the heart."

Matters of the heart. I had not heard anyone other than the older people say that.

"That means you do have feelings for me?"

"Look Milena, I think you're a smart young girl who has a lot to offer any man that you fall in love with. I just don't think I am that man."

He walked close to the balcony where the stench was emanating from. He crinkled his nose at the smell. Outside, the day was coming to its end, and the shadows of the building across the street were no longer clear and distinguishable. The rotten smell, the result of the dead dove that had probably been sacrificed to scare off the previous family, permeated throughout.

"I just can't...."

"You can't have anything serious with me because I'm a jinetera?" I said finishing his sentence.

"Milena, it's got nothing to do with what you've done," he said, turning around to face me. "I just want you to do what your heart tells you to, not what you think you ought to."

"I am doing what my heart tells me."

"Now you're lying."

"I'm not," I said. "You've made it clear that I don't have to re-pay you for anything you've done for me, so no, it is not the idea of being indebted to you."

"Then what is it? I can't imagine that at your age, you find an old man like me attractive."

"I like how you just know everything. How you walk into places and people notice you, how you take charge of everything around you."

"You're impressed, you don't really like me."

"I thought to like someone they had to impress you first."

"You're still just at the impression state, like a crush on a teacher." He put both hands on my shoulders and squeezed them, kept his eyes on mine.

"Martin," I said exhaling, "They're going to find me. Kristen will be sent back to the family who killed her mother, and I'll go to jail. I need to leave La Habana."

"To Miami?"

"Miami ultimately. Matanzas first."

"Matanzas? Why?"

"Herman has a house there, and I can..."

There was another knock on the door. He released my shoulders.

"Don't tell me," he said. "I don't need to know, I'm not getting involved."

"But you said when I turn eighteen...?"

"I'm going to be in La Habana taking care of my businesses. If you're still here in a year, then..."

"How will you find me? What if I'm not here?"

He gave me a wide smile. "If it's meant to be, it will be. I have to go now," he said walking toward the door.

When he opened it, Herman had his hands full of bags. Herman walked in, dropped the bags on the table, and started to wash his hands. I stood motionless, unsettled by Martin's actions, his insufficient interest in me, by the prospect of escape on my own.

"He wants nothing to do with me," I said, taking one of the two chairs in the kitchen.

"Looks like you got yourself in some serious trouble and you're going to have to get out on your own," he said, taking the other chair.

"I don't know anyone in Matanzas? I..."

"I can help with the house, but..."

"What I really need is to get out of the country."

"That can be arranged from anywhere. Don't you think people from Cardenas and Jaguey Grande leave on rafts like people from La Habana do?"

"I don't want to take Kristen on a raft."

"You have to if you want to get out of here."

"My mother didn't take me."

"You don't have anyone to leave her with."

"I'm not going to leave her. I just don't want to leave on a raft."

"Milena, you know that unless someone marries you..."

"I know," I said interrupting.

The baby complained from the bed. She was dry but hungry and wailed even as I picked her up to rock her. In the kitchen with her in one arm, I poured the powdered milk and mixed the water into the brand new baby bottle Herman had somehow procured. Kristen was fidgety and would not take the bottle; she had stopped the loud wailing, but continued to sob. I didn't know what to do with her. My cousins had been able to feed themselves, and go to the bathroom on their own. I realized all this time, I had not had a thought about them, and wondered how their mother was treating them now that she had no one to watch them anymore.

I tried everything for the baby to take the milk, but nothing worked. I couldn't imagine that someone had breastfed her since her mother had died. And I didn't think Kassandra had breastfed for too long either. I know from experience that when you're hungry, taste doesn't matter. So it couldn't be that she didn't like the raspy consistency of the powdered milk. I tried pouring some of the milk onto the back of my wrist, like I had seen mothers do, to test the temperature. Nothing came out. No wonder she wasn't eating, the plastic nipple had no hole.

I looked in all the drawers of the kitchen for a pair of scissors. No luck. With my right fang, I took a tiny bite of the nipple, and stuck it in her mouth. She sucked and sucked and finally calmed down. Sitting on the couch with her feeding in my arms, I couldn't deny that the decision to take care of Kristen had been more a reason to save myself. Now, this tiny, defenseless creature depended solely on me.

It wasn't long before the bottle was empty and

Kristen was dozing off in my arms. I lay down on the couch, put her on my chest to sleep. Her breath, shallow and short smelled of sour milk. The skin on her tiny fingers was starting to peel off. Her face was peaceful, happy, like my aunt used to say: a full stomach means a happy baby. She opened her eyes momentarily and stared at me. I felt guilty, as if she had somehow known what was going through my head. I ran my hand by the back of her head and started to whisper a lullaby. She continued to stare, but soon, her eyes gave in and she fell asleep.

I, too, soon fell into a light sleep only to dream of my mother drowning in the huge sea, screaming out for me to swim, for me to hang on to something. I couldn't see myself in the dream, but in the distance, a small human figure kept batting its arms at the ocean.

I awoke feeling cold, disoriented and out of breath. Kristen yawned on my bosom; her breath a rush of warm air bringing me back to reality. Immediately, I felt the coldness in my torso. I lifted the baby to find my shirt soaked in urine, and from the balcony door, the darkness of my first night alone with her.

When I was changing her, she started to cry again. I heard the nurse's warning of how troublesome premature babies can be. I tried feeding her again, but she didn't take the bottle. I walked around the house with her, I sang, I rocked. Nothing seemed to calm her until I lied on the couch and put her in my bosom again. She did not fall asleep, but simply stared up at me with those big green eyes that were identical to

Kassandra's.

"Do you miss her?" I asked in a whisper.

She started to cry again, her answer to my un-discreet question, I suppose. Soon she quieted down, only to start crying again shortly thereafter when someone knocked on the door. I could not pretend to not hear the second or third knock as each was getting increasingly louder. I hurried to the bedroom with Kristen wailing. In the middle of the bed was the pacifier. I stuck it in her mouth and rocked her side to side vigorously. The knocks kept coming; now in the company of Helen's demanding voice saying she knew I was there, she could hear the baby.

Kristen stopped crying, and although she wasn't ready for more sleep, I put her down on the bed between the pillows, then ran to the door. Helen was fuming.

"Why did it take you so long to open the door?"

"Didn't you hear the baby?"

"I need to leave quickly so let me in," she demanded as she pushed past me into the hall. I closed the door hastily, wanting really bad to tell her off for pushing me. But didn't. It couldn't be good for me to confront Helen right now about her rough edges. After all, mine weren't too polished either. I had begun to notice how she had become more crude in her ways, more like the mercenary style of a Cuban woman in full survival mode. I, on the other hand, strived to compose myself, to behave like she would in my situation. It was an eerie reversal I had to welcome.

I went to check on Kristen, who miraculously was

not making a peep.

"Excuse me," I said, walking back into the narrow stretch that was the kitchen, the hall and half the living room. "But I had to check on her. Did you bring the money?"

"Look at you! All business, huh?"

"Why else would you be here, Helen? You don't care what happens to me unless Martin cares."

"Listen, you little shit," she said furiously with her index finger declaring war. "I've done nothing but help you, from the jail where I found you to this house. So you better think twice what you say to me, you hear?"

"Only because that's what Martin pays you to do," I said, toning it down a bit.

"You've got a mouth on you lately."

"Survival," I said, praying silently for some comraderie with her new self.

"You think you know about survival?" she yelled. "You've had everyone running around for you! You don't know what real surviving is!"

"I don't?" now I was raising my voice, too. "Try being raped by two cops, or having a coked up freaked out guy smack the shit out of you, or have your mother drown and your friend jump to her death. How's surviving all that!"

Helen was quiet, held the threat of my stare without a flinch. Then broke down into hysterical laughs. I couldn't help but do the same. We laughed like kids do when they discover how simple something is.

"I'm sorry," she said after a pause.

"For what? Being rude?"

"Because I refused to help you."

"I know you need to protect your job."

"That's not all, Milena. I have a lot of my own money invested with Martin. I know people think I just do the leg work for him, but in fact, many of the investments he has in the island are partly mine as well."

"I didn't know that."

"Not a lot of people do. They just think I'm his personal assistant. But we're partners; not in all of the businesses he has but some."

"How many does he have?"

"A considerable amount. Plus he has plans to invest in more; he wants to own most of this city within the next five years."

"Own most of the city?"

The concept of private ownership had been eliminated by the Revolution in 1960. No one was allowed personal property including real estate, and even American businessmen who had been residing in Cuba for a long time, had been stripped of all their belongings. Now, in the midst of the Special Period, foreigners could own anything from private homes to hotels, something Cubans couldn't even dream of.

"Cuba is going to change a lot in the next few years. With Russia unable to help now, Castro is going to appeal to international investors for money. He's already succumbing to capitalism, and he'll have to continue to do so if he wants to stay in power."

"You're speaking another language."

"I know, sorry."

"I understand what capitalism is, and I don't think Fidel will ever let that happen."

"He already has."

I was confused. In all my years of schooling the one thing that was constant was the idea that capitalism was the Devil incarnate, and we were the only country in the world that had not fallen prey to it. And for that, we had to be thankful to the Revolution.

"Didn't you get paid in dollars only?" Helen said sitting on one of the two chairs in the small kitchen. "Don't you have to buy everything with dollars nowadays? What do you think that's called?"

"But that's not what we've been taught."

"Your generation knows nothing other than the Revolution and now this ridiculous Special Period. You are really young and naïve and have lots to learn still."

"I'm not that naïve anymore."

"So you think," she said running her hand through her hair. "I wish I still believed, too."

"Believed what? I don't think you're so cynical."

We smiled at each other. Helen was full of cynicism, about her personal as well as professional life. She didn't make any attempts at hiding it. Anyone who dealt with her also knew this.

"Thanks," she said, getting up from the chair to walk to the balcony. Then she opened the sliding door and the foul smell waltzed its way into the house. I followed her out. Although it was officially night time, the heat was almost the same it had been at noon. We stood there, silently feeling the drops of sweat run down our backs as we looked down at the dead dove. The humidity was high, but not a breeze ran through the neglected city, not even on a second floor.

"Bring me a broom and a bag." She commanded.

I ran inside to do what I was told. I could not bring myself to pick up the dead bird for fear some brujeria had been done to it. But Helen didn't believe in anything, not even in the power of evil.

She swept the dead bird into the bag, handed it to me, and went inside to wash her hands in the sink. I knotted the bag, threw it down on top of the closed dumpster underneath the balcony, and went inside to do the same.

"I wish I could go with you, wherever you go." She said drying her hands.

"So that's why Martin doesn't want to get involved with me. He doesn't want to leave Cuba." I started on the topic again.

"Not yet anyway."

"You think he ever will?"

"Eventually. But not right now. He might return to visit his family but..."

"His family? He told me he didn't have any?"

Helen took a deep breath and let it out slowly. She put both hands on the edge of the sink, and let her head drop between her shoulders.

"Milena, sit down," she said turning around to face me. I obeyed.

"Martin had twin daughters. They died in an airplane crash on their way to university in the United States."

I was stunned, dizzy with incomprehension, unable to muster a word.

"His wife is in an asylum in Quebec."

"She's not dead?" I managed to ask.

"No, she's not dead."

"He didn't tell me anything about her or his daughters."

"Why would he?"

"I'm not just anyone. I think he cares for me."

"He does, but you are two years younger than his daughters were when they died. He can't bring himself to accepting that."

"One year."

"Whatever. The point is you're too young."

"He didn't have a problem with that when we met at the malecon." I said, savoring the truth.

"He thought you were older and it was just going to be a one night thing. Martin cares what happens to you but he's not going to risk anything for you."

"That's caring?"

"Listen, he wanted to help you by giving you the opportunity to run the restaurant. You're young, you're pretty, and you're Cuban. It was a perfect business deal."

"It was all just business?"

"For the most part."

"He never would've married me and taken me out of here, huh?"

"Did he ever tell you he would?"

"No," I said, looking down.

"He asked me to tell you the truth."

"Why didn't he tell me himself?"

"I guess he just didn't want to hurt you."

"So he sends someone to do it?"

"That's how he handles most things."

There was a short silence between us. I didn't know if I thought Martin a hero or a coward.

"He should have told me about his wife."

"You should've told him your real age. You shouldn't be angry with him."

"I'm not angry, I'm disappointed."

"Get used to it," she said patting my back. "That's why I don't date men. Sooner or later, they disappoint you."

Her comment made me think of my mother and her ordeal with my father; of Kassandra and the self-destructive love she once felt for Camacho, of all the love stories I'd watch my mother's friends go through, and of the few that ended happily.

"Listen, what I said earlier about everyone running around for you? You're on your own. No one's going to be with you in Matanzas."

"I don't know anyone in Matanzas."

"Herman does. He asked me to give you this." She handed me an envelope as I sat up. In it was a piece of paper with an address, and a brand new identification card with a 1974 birth-date.

"With that," she pointed to the card in my hand, "you can work anywhere and save up to hire a boat to take you both to Miami."

"But a boat will cost a lot of money and I can't..."

"I'm giving you enough for a couple of months rent

and some food," she said, dropping two neat stacks of dollars on the table. "You're gonna have to figure out the rest."

For a split second, I could see a flash of tenderness in her eyes, like an unwilling passenger in a runaway train.

"I'm scared," I said.

"It's reasonable to be scared," Helen answered. "But you're going to be okay."

"You didn't think I should leave before. Why now?"

"Because frankly, you've become a liability to everyone."

"What about going in front of a judge?

"Don't worry about that. If you're gone, who are they going to prosecute?"

"All this time you kept me thinking I'd end up in jail."

"You still might if you stay here."

"I didn't kill my friend, Helen."

"I know."

"Those people forced her to drink something rotten; I could smell it when I got back in the room through the window."

"Herman told me, Milena. You don't need to."

"I do. I want them to pay for what they did."

"Tell me where they live." Helen said looking down at her shoes.

I gave her the address to Padrino's house, and told her that's where she would probably find Camacho, sooner or later. She said she would see about taking care of it.

I didn't feel as happy as I thought I would to know that Camacho, Padrino and the old lady would get what they deserved. Instead, a piercing sadness for my mother, my friend, my life, filled me and all I could do was cry.

"No reason to cry now," Helen said reverting to her usual tough skin. "You took this baby, you have to leave the city now to protect her."

"Then what?" I said, wiping my cheek with the back of my hand.

"Then you go to that address," she said, pointing at the piece of paper.

"Do they know I'm coming?"

"Yes, but you know how things are. You have to find a job and blend in as much as you can quickly. You might want to think about finding your father in Miami."

"My father?"

"He's the only relative you've got in the United States."

"But he never wanted anything to do with me. Why would he now?"

"Sometimes, people regret what they've done."

"If he had, wouldn't he have helped my mother when she was trying to leave?"

"Maybe now he feels guilty and he will help his daughter. I don't know Milena, but you have to try because if you make it to the United States things are very difficult over there. You don't speak the language, you'll be all alone. You can't do the same thing you did for a living here!"

"I don't ever want to do that again anywhere!"

"Then you need to at least try to contact your father. If he doesn't want to help you, "she said throwing her hands up, "then it's on him. But it will be easier if he does."

The idea of finding my father had not even crossed my mind. I couldn't feel anything but resentment towards him. My mother had raised me on her own without ever asking for anything other than for me to have his last name. And even that he'd denied her. Why now he would help me was beyond my comprehension.

"What about Kassandra's mother?" I asked.

"What about her?"

"Lucia told me she lives in Europe."

"Milena, think about how big Europe is. How would you even begin to look for her?"

I knew she was right.

"You leave tomorrow."

"Tomorrow? But Herman said the house won't be ready until the end of the month?"

"You need to find somewhere to stay meanwhile. You can't stay in La Habana."

"Is he going with me?'

"Kristen is going with you. You and the baby, that's it. They're going to come asking us questions, and we're going to say you just took off. But if they somehow find out about this house, with you and the baby in it, we're all done."

I took a deep breath to try to slow my heart down. Its pounding resonating throughout my body reaching my head, where it became louder.

"I suggest you get a good night sleep. Herman will come back tomorrow to drop you off at the train station."

I nodded in agreement, stood to walk her to the door.

"I guess tonight is a good a night to pray to pray to the orishas, to the saints and everything else you believe in." She said trying to be funny.

We both laughed, not as hysterical as we had before, but a laugh that leaves an invisible scar of sadness. I knew I would never see Helen again, or Martin, or the city of my childhood. However, the prospect of finding my father made me more nervous than escaping from Cuba on a clandestine boat with a baby that wasn't mine. Fatherly feelings arise from raising the child, not because it is innate in men, I remembered my mother saying. The few men in my life had not demonstrated otherwise, starting with my neighbor who had used me for sex, to Martin, who cared but not enough. It wasn't anger I felt, just utter disappointment. I had believed the fact that Martin helped me meant he truly cared; this is where Helen was right I guess, about me being naïve. Now I see there are degrees of caring. People could care about something, like the Cuban people cared, at one point, about their Revolution. And then, after some rough patches and high waters, people stopped caring. My father, who had cared about my mother, but not enough to risk everything, was the only person I had to look for in Miami. If someone cares but not enough, do they really care? Helen said she didn't know the answer to that. She didn't know the answers to many questions about my leave, just advised me to follow my instincts. I told her I felt I couldn't trust my instincts; they obviously couldn't tell left from right when it came to people and their motives.

Before Helen left that night, she gave me two aspirins and a quick hug. I fed Kristen one more time, and changed her again before falling asleep next to her, listening to her short breaths with my arms around her. Knowing that I had someone to protect now gave me just a slight inkling into what my mother must have felt when she made the decision to leave without me in order to protect me.

I dreamt of the time she and I rode the ferry from Regla to La Habana to visit my aunt. I was seven years old and the santera that lived next door had told me I was a daughter of La Virgen de Regla, and that I should make an offering to her anytime I was in the water. So I took the gold bracelet my mother's mother had given her, and that she had put on my left wrist just before leaving the house that afternoon, and threw it in the water as the ferry left the bay. My mother was furious with me for hanging half my body out of the boat to release the jewelry to the ocean. She said she didn't believe in those things, and what if I would've fallen into the water, and a shark would have eaten me, and how that gold bracelet was the only thing she had from her mother. Now, I prayed Yemaya would remember my innocent offering ten years before, and that in exchange she would keep Kristen and me safe in her waters.

ABOUT THE AUTHOR

YOUSI MAZPULE is a professor of English at Johnson & Wales University. She has an MFA in Creative Writing and has been published in several magazines including *Generation ñ*, *Prick of the Spindle*, *Nanofiction* and *Coral Gables Living*. *Jinetera* is her first novel. She lives in Miami, FL.

Made in United States
North Haven, CT
21 April 2023

35720012R00134